From where he sat at the edge of the bar, Kyle had a great view. He raised his eyebrow at Craig, who kept on polishing a glass without giving the two newcomers more than a glance and a friendly hello. Craig was like that; he didn't judge anyone unless they were causing trouble in his bar, and these two weren't. Yet. They came right up to the bar, the kid looking sulky and the cowboy looking as pleased as could be.

With one hand on the pretty dolly's back, the cowboy nodded, his hat brim dipping low, and grinned right at Craig. He rumbled, low and smooth, "You order a drink, baby. I'll be right back." He didn't wait for a reply, but took a fast look around and headed to the bathrooms.

"Yeah, sure, Chet. I'll do that." The kid, who actually looked a lot older close up, didn't sound overly pleased.

Cowboy Chet either didn't care or didn't notice. He walked past Kyle, still grinning happily, and tipped his hat again. Kyle had to assume he hadn't heard. The man was too damn cheerful to let his boyfriend's attitude ride.

Kyle smiled right back at him, liking the guy's eyes even if he did have lousy taste in men. Kyle checked out the view from the other side, too, not caring if the whiny half of the pair saw him or not. If it came to it, Kyle knew he could take out the kid with one solid punch.

Cowboy Chet had a stellar ass, all dressed up in nice, tight Wranglers.

The Five O'Clock Bar
TOP SHELF
An imprint of Torquere Press Publishers
PO Box 2545
Round Rock, TX 78680
Copyright © 2008 by Sean Michael, Chris Owen, Julia Talbot, and BA Tortuga
Cover illustration by A. Squires
Published with permission
ISBN: 978-1-60370-549-3, 1-60370-549-X

www.torquerepress.com

First Torquere Press Printing: December 2008
Printed in the USA

**If you enjoyed The Five O'Clock Bar,
you might enjoy these Torquere Press titles:**

Bareback by Chris Owen

The Broken Road by Sean Michael

Jumping into Things by Julia Talbot

Long Road Home by BA Tortuga

The Five O'Clock Bar

The Five O'Clock Bar by Sean Michael,
Chris Owen, Julia Talbot and BA Tortuga

Torquere
Press
Inc.
romance for the rest of us
www.torquerepress.com

The Five O'Clock Bar

Table of Contents

The Five O'Clock Bar

Owner of the Five O'Clock
by Sean Michael

"Last call! Last call for alcohol!" Craig reached up and rang the big brass bell under the old clock above the bar, the sound cutting through the music from the jukebox, the laughter over by the pool tables, and the fight that was trying to start at the edge of the dance floor. Twinks. Fucking save him.

"Bob, honey? Go break that shit up for me? Hank and Lew are going kill each other over that slimy little whore. Kid was fucking Jimmy not four hours ago in the men's room."

The big, beautiful cop nodded, flexed for him and waded in, the crowd breaking up just like that.

Man, that was too damn cool.

Craig poured out beers and whiskey, three vodka and tonics, four margaritas, and a salty dog, whistling happily. Had to love a busy Thursday night. It boded well for the weekend take.

"Hey, barkeep, am I too late to get a whiskey shooter and a beer?"

He turned at the question and saw Barney sitting there,

large as life, looking tired but happy.

"Almost. Luckily, I know the owner." He leaned over the bar for a quick kiss hello, Frankie and Oliver hooting and clapping for them. Then he pulled a Bud for Barney and poured two fingers of Jack.

Barney's smile was warm, the look in those eyes even warmer as they slid over him in a way he'd been missing the last six days.

Bad weather had extended Barney's latest run by over two days.

"Good to be home?" Craig started packing up the garnishes. The snacks were already squared away and the crowds were slowly heading out.

"Shit, yes. That snow storm up north nearly killed me. Bumper to fucking bumper for nearly two days straight."

Barney shot back the whiskey, throat working, the shot glass tiny in that beefy hand.

"You home for the holidays?" He stacked shot glasses and got them in the little Hobart to wash even as he nodded to a couple of leather daddies who dumped money in the tip jar.

"I am. Got a little tree in the cab." Barney tilted his head side to side, cracking his neck. "A thing or two in a box, too."

"Good." Craig pushed his ponytail back over his shoulder, the whole thing wrapped in a leather sheath while he was working. "All I have to do is close up and count money and we can head to the house."

"You want me to hurry the stragglers on out, babe?" Barney drained his beer mug and stood, broad shoulders and thick chest testament to his strength.

"Between you and Bob, you could clear it out..." Craig's prick jumped a little.

"Anything to hurry you up." Barney gave him a wink

and moved on down to the bar, clapping the big cop on the shoulder. "What do you say, man? Gonna help me empty this place out so Craig can close up?"

"You know it, cutie. I need to get home to my man. Doc's pulling doubles this week so we can go to Vermont for Christmas."

"Yeah? I'm done 'til the New Year. Told dispatch not to disturb me. I've paid my dues, you know?"

Barney and Bob started moving everyone out, nobody willing to argue with the two hard bodies pushing them toward the door.

Craig turned the key and started running totals, dancing a little over the thought of Barn home for almost three straight weeks.

He wasn't going to be able to walk straight.

Like Barn had heard him, the man looked over from the front door, grinning at him, eyes hot even at this distance. Craig grinned back, gave his man a nod. Sexy man.

The last drunk was escorted out by Bob, the big cop giving him a wave and a shouted "goodnight." Barn locked the door up behind them, shooting the bars at the top and bottom of the door home before coming back his way.

"Is it still snowing?" Craig asked. Not like it mattered. His house was built on the land behind the bar, quiet and simple and far enough back no one looked for it.

"Yeah, it is. Really coming down, too. I'm glad I'm done 'til the New Year. I'd hate to be out in another storm like the one I just came through." Barn shook his head and reached up, grinned. "I'm looking forward to a warm bed tonight with plenty of room to stretch out on." Not that the man would. It didn't matter how big the bed was, Barn would wrap tight around him.

"I'm looking forward to walking bowlegged tomorrow

and having the guys tease me." No sense beating around the bush.

"Fuck, yes." Barn laughed and reached across the bar to wrap one large hand around Craig's neck, tugging him to meet Barn halfway, his mouth taken in a hard, deep welcome-me-home kiss.

Craig crawled up over the bar, just pushing into Barn's arms. Home. Home. Home. Barn groaned, arms wrapping around him, tugging him in against the muscled chest.

"Babe."

"Yeah." Yeah. Take him. Now. Here. Hot. "Door's locked."

"You got anything slick behind that bar of yours?" Barn grabbed his ass, squeezed his cheeks nice and hard and pulled him up close so he could feel exactly why Barn might need the slick. His lover's cock was hard behind his jeans.

"I... Booze makes a lousy lube."

"We can do it the old fashioned way." Barn licked his lips, made his eyebrows go up and down, hands working his jeans off as nice as you please.

"Oh. Oh, fuck. This is... dirty." Hot.

"Is not — I watched you wipe down the bar." Grinning, Barn took another kiss as his jeans were tugged down past Craig's hips. He pushed into the kiss, fucking Barn's lips with his tongue, just going to town.

Complaining a little, Barn broke the kiss and turned him, kicking Craig's feet apart as far as his jeans would let them go, one solid hand pushing in the middle of his back, bending him over his bar.

"I've missed you." It wasn't a constant, really, but when he didn't get his lover on schedule, it tugged at him.

"I know. I've been dreaming of this ass." His big tough truck driver went down on his knees, right there in the bar, and licked at Craig's crack, giving a happy little hum.

"Barn." Ten years together — ten years — and it still rocked.

"You taste good, babe. Taste like home." He got another little hum and then thick fingers spread his ass cheeks wide, Barn's tongue concentrating on wetting his hole, outside and in.

"Yeah. Need you. Need you in me, yeah?" They were going to have to bleach the bar.

"Fuck, yes." Barney rose up, rubbing the head of that fat prick against his ass.

He pushed back, just taking Barn's cock in.

"Craig!" Barn's hands grabbed hold of his hips and tugged him on back farther. "Shit, that's good. That's good."

"Good. Love. Love, damn." Riding up and down felt perfect, caused his toes to curl.

Barn, leaned over him some, body warm against his back, teeth sinking into his neck, right above the collar of his T-shirt.

"Mmm." He loved to wear Barn's mark. Really.

Biting turned to sucking, Barn keeping time with his thrusts, a zing flying between the two sensations. Barney hummed against his skin, the vibration making him shiver. Making his balls draw up tight.

"God, I fucking love this. Love coming home to you." One of Barn's hands slid around to find Craig's cock, taking it, holding it, jacking it.

"Oh. Oh, there. Yeah. Home. Damn, lover." His toes curled and he moaned, wanting more.

Barn's words faded to grunts and moans as his lover shifted slightly and fucked him harder, faster, managing to find his gland in the process. Yes! His balls drew up and his eyes flew open, seed spraying from him.

"Shit, yes!" Barn shouted for him, loud and happy. His lover humped into him a few more times and then heat filled him deep inside.

"Mmm. Barn. Welcome home."

Barn kissed the back of his neck, lips warm and soft where he'd bitten. "Thanks, babe."

"Mmmhmm. There's snacks up at the house. Good coffee." A huge tub. Their bed.

"What kind of snacks?" Barn asked, groaning as his softening cock slid out of Craig's body. Barn's fingers slid over the backs of his thighs, rubbing in the come.

"Uh... Chex Mix. Pretzels. Meatballs."

"Oh, meatballs." Barn reached around and grabbed his testicles.

"Mmmhmm. Meaty-ballies..." He wiggled a little, laughing as it tugged.

Barn laughed, body shifting against his. Then Barn turned him, smiling into his eyes. "You made me meatballs? The ones with the garlic?"

"I did. They're in the crockpot on low." Because he was a kickass boyfriend.

"Damn, you're good to me." Barn's lips slid slowly over his as those big hands carefully tucked him back into his jeans.

"I love you, you big lug. Let's go home."

Barn chuckled and nodded. "Yeah, babe. Me, too." Barn slung an arm around his shoulders. "Tomorrow we're coming in early and putting up some decorations."

"We are?" Craig leaned in, locked up, shuddering at the wind. "You'll have to help me pull the boxes down."

Barn rubbed his arm, hurrying them along the path back to the house. "You've got your pack mule for three weeks, babe. Use me as you will." The corner of Barney's lips twitched. "Please, babe, use me."

"You know I will. Hell, I have *plans* for you."

"Oh, I like the sound of that." Barn bumped their hips together. "What plans?"

"Sex. Dancing. Christmas morning waffles. Midnight kisses."

"Those sound like good plans, babe. I have packages in the truck. Presents and stuff. We'll get them tomorrow, too. Right now? Coffee, meatballs and you, yeah?"

"Yeah. Coffee. Meatballs. Me." Craig bounced like a teenager.

Barn swatted his ass as they walked into their home. "Oh, fuck, babe. Smells good."

"Home, home." Craig leaned up, stole a kiss. "I'm going to get cleaned up; you want some sweats?"

Grabbing hold of his ass, Barn squeezed it, tugged him in close. "I want to be part of the clean-up. It sounds... dirty."

Craig's cheeks went hot, bright red. "Shower? Bath?" They had a little attachment on the shower head for cleaning...

"Shower." Barn's fingers slid over the seam of his jeans, pushing it into his crack.

"Barn." He went up on tiptoe.

"Right here, babe."

"I..." Right. Moving. Walking. Going to the bathroom. He could *feel* Barn watching his ass as he headed down the hallway. He made sure to shake it the whole way.

"Someone's asking for it." And didn't Barn sound like he wanted to give!

"Yeah. Yeah, Barney. I'm more than asking."

"You'll get it, babe."

Those big hands helped him take his clothes off, pushing up his T-shirt and undoing his jeans for the second time in less than an hour.

The bathroom was their second big indulgence, after the bedroom and their bed. From the tiles to the huge tub to the glass walled shower, this was a good place. Barn flipped the lights, switching the over head for the recessed lights by the shower. Then the towel warmer was turned on, Barn putting the biggest, fluffiest towels they had on it.

"Come on, babe. Get that water going and I'll take care of you."

"You got it." It didn't take long for the steam to start, water splashing on the tiles.

Barn crowded him into the cubicle, the wide shower head spraying a large enough swath of water that they both got wet. "Shit, this might be what I miss the most on the road." Barn swatted his ass gently. "Aside from your ass, that is."

"Ah, to be outdone by a shower with attachments..." Craig swatted back, laughing under his breath. Asshole.

"Hey, I said *aside* from your ass. That means you do edge out the shower." Barn grinned down at him. "Just."

"Oh, man. Given that I'm way older than the shower, that's good, right?"

"You're like a fine wine, babe. You get better as you age." Barn suddenly swatted his ass again. "Enough with the sap already — you know I'm glad to be home — let's get soapy."

"Soapy it is." He grabbed the Irish Spring, the green bar sudsing right on up, the smell making him hum a little.

Barn stole some of the suds, running slick hands over his body. "Gonna clean you inside and out, babe."

Craig didn't answer, just focused on washing and rubbing bubbles over Barn's chest, fingers sliding over the mat of soft hair.

"Love your touch," murmured Barn, hands continuing to move over him, fingers rubbing his belly and then dropping lower to slide soapily up and down his prick.

"Mmm." Craig kept touching, too, eyes rolling back in his head.

Barn's touch moved to his balls, cupping, squeezing, rolling them with those big, soapy fingers. One finger slipped back, touching his hole for just a second. Just enough to be a promise. Craig spread a little, moaned a little more. He could still feel the stretch from before.

"When's the last time we cleaned you inside, babe?"

"I..." His cheeks went hot, lips lifted up for a kiss. "September? Before?"

"Oh, man. That's just not right." Barn's touches became firmer, sliding over his skin and helping the water wash away the soap.

"Mmm. You're something." Craig let himself relax, let himself melt into Barn's touch.

"That's why you kept me all those years ago, huh?"

"One of them. I have a lot."

"Yeah?" It wasn't like Barn to fish for compliments, but he'd been gone nearly a week and they'd only had a day between this last run and the one before it.

"Yeah." He leaned in, hands massaging Barn's back. "Mainly it was your laugh. You fucking laughed in the bar that first night and I was hard and fucking fascinated."

Barn chuckled and nuzzled their cheeks together. "You still get hard when we laugh together."

"I do. Nobody does happy like you, Barn. Nobody."

One big hand started massaging his ass. "I'm pretty happy right now, babe."

"God, I am, too. Almost three weeks of full-time stud muffin." And there was that laugh, right on cue. It came with a finger pushing into him, sliding in to the first knuckle and wriggling. "Barney." He spread, eyes trying to roll a little bit.

"I'll take care of you, babe, you know that." Pushing

deep for a second, that finger was soon gone, and Barn grabbed the shower head, working on the special attachment.

"I. Damn. Barn..." Kinky, hungry, fine bastard. His stomach was just vibrating.

"Just look at you, Craig. You're already fucking glowing and we haven't even really started yet."

"Yeah, well. I got this need..."

"What you've got is an itch and I know just how to scratch it." Barn got the attachment onto the showerhead, turned the spigot so the flow of water stopped.

When Barn's eyes met his, there was a whole lot of need there, too. His belly went tight, a deep groan escaping him.

Barn rubbed his belly, and then that hand slipped around to rub his lower back. "Turn around and bend for me, babe."

"I... Yeah. Yeah, man." Craig turned, put his hands on the tile.

"Mmm..." Barney's hands slid up along either side of his spine, and then back down, the movements slow and easy, Barn taking his time. Craig groaned, head falling forward. So good. So hot. Those hands landed on his ass, massaging, spreading him. Barn's thumbs slid along his crack and then pushed at his hole, spreading him open.

"Love you, huh?" He did. Really.

"I know, babe." A kiss landed at the base of his spine, Barney's lips hot on his skin, on that bundle of nerves that shot the sensations from Barn's tongue dancing on his skin all through his body. He spread a little wider, went up on his toes. "You're so fucking ready for this." Those thumbs spread him again, pushing in a little deeper this time before disappearing.

Craig didn't have a good answer, so he whimpered, protesting the loss of that touch.

Barn stroked his back. "Easy now. I'm just getting the tubing, yeah?" Then his ass cheeks were spread again and one of Barn's fingers guided the tube into his body.

"Yeah..." The nozzle at the end was shaped like a plug, the metal warming inside him. Barn turned and twisted it, waking up any nerves that weren't already working overtime. He couldn't keep still, couldn't stop jerking and rocking and moving.

"Yeah, that's it, babe. Move for me. Show me how much you love it." One of Barn's fingers slid in alongside the nozzle.

"Barn!" Oh. Oh, fuck. Hot. Full.

"I love how tight you are, babe. So fucking smooth and pretty inside." His Barn was an ass man — always had been.

"Touch me. Fuck. The stuff I want..." Barn made him nuts.

That finger inside him circled around the plug shaped nozzle. ""Tell me. Tell me what you want."

"You. Your touch. Filling me up. Want you." He loved his life, loved his bar, his house, his land. All of it paled next to his Barney.

"You want my hand when we're done with the cleaning, babe? Want to feel my fist fucking you?"

"Barney." Fuck. Fuck him. Had it only been an hour ago he was slinging suds?

"Mmm. I think you do." Barn's finger slid away, Craig's body snapping closed around the plug.

He gasped, went up on his tip toes. Damn.

"Here it comes, Craig. Here comes the water." Barn fiddled with the taps and a slow stream of water began to fill him.

He groaned, fingers curling heart starting to pound. "Oh. Oh, fuck me."

"I did. And I will again." Barn chuckled, rubbing his

lower back as the water kept filling him.

"P...promise?" Oh, fuck. He. Damn...

"Never doubt it, babe. Not for a fucking second."

"Never." He leaned back, letting Barney comfort him, love on him.

Those warm fingers slid around to rub his belly, easing the muscles there. "Almost full, babe. Almost time to stop."

"Full. Fuck, Barn. No more room." No more.

"Shh. Shh. I've got you, babe." Barn kissed the back of his neck. "I won't let you explode."

His head feel forward, eyes closing. Yeah. Exploding would be bad.

Another kiss warmed his skin and then Barn turned off the water. "I'm taking it out now, babe." One hand still stroking his belly, Barn slowly, carefully tugged the nozzle from his body.

He panted, eyes closed, shaking good and hard. Barn stayed close, petting his belly, nuzzling his spine, breath hot and sweet against his skin. He slowly relaxed, slowly accepted the pressure, the heat inside him.

"There you go, that's it." Barn's voice was soft and warm and full of pride, passion. "Let me just get the shower running again, babe."

"I hate this part."

"There's no reason to," murmured Barney, getting the shower head re-attached, the hot water coming back on and pouring over them.

"Yeah. This is... you know." Almost too intimate.

Barn's hands moved him, turned him so his face pressed into Barn's chest. "It's okay, babe. Just let go and I'll hold you and after I'll soap you up one more time and take you to bed."

It wasn't ever that easy, but he managed to relax, to let it happen. To trust this to his Barn. And Barney didn't make a big deal of it at all. When he was empty again, those big hands moved over him, soapy, slick and warm.

"Barney. Kiss me." Please.

"I can do that. Here?" Barn kissed his shoulder, mouth open over the ball, tongue sliding on his skin. Then Barn moved to his nipple. "What about here?" Barn's mouth was so fucking hot.

"Yes. Yes, more."

"Mmm..." The vibrations of the sound spread out along his skin, and then Barn spread little kisses all up along his shoulder and neck until their mouths pressed hotly together.

Craig moaned, tongue fucking Barney's lips, cock aching. Barney squeezed his ass while they kissed, fingers teasing at his hole, rubbing it, stroking it. Sensitive. Damn. Just. Wow.

"Mmm... we'd best move this to the bedroom. I don't plan on you being able to stand on those legs by the time I'm done with you."

"Promises, promises." Fuck him, yes.

Barn chuckled, broad chest moving against him. "You know I'm good for it."

"I do. Thank God. Come on, you big lug. Bed."

"Yes."

Barn turned off the water and grabbed a towel, warm from the heated rack, drying him off with more speed than sensuality. Someone was eager to move things along. And if the hurried toweling off hadn't been clue enough, the way Barn's cock bobbed and swayed, trying to get his attention, was. He gave it attention, too, hand wrapping around it, pulling nice and strong while Barn rubbed him.

"Fuck, babe, you're gonna make me blow again." Barn's voice was nice and rough, that edge of need right there.

"Am I?" Craig squeezed again, then tugged, moving them to the bed.

"You are." Barn goosed him as they got there, making him jump and fall into the bed. "Ah, now I've got you just where I want you."

He was up on his hands and knees, rocking, making a clear offer. He was all about the wanting.

"Sexy, Craig. You are so fucking sexy."

Barn detoured around the bed to grab the lube and then settled behind him, warm and solid, hands touching the backs of his thighs, his ass cheeks, his balls.

"You want me like this, Barn?" He spread a little, getting settled, getting comfortable.

"This will work." A soft kiss landed on his right ass cheek. "I'd like to see your face while I do it, but it's up to you, babe."

"Mmm." That made him blush a little, made him feel sexy as fuck, so he turned, let Barn put a couple of pillows under his ass.

Barn's heavy gaze slid up over his body, stopping when their eyes met. "You're gonna be walking funny tomorrow, babe."

"I hope so. I hope I look incredibly well-fucked."

"You will be — whether you look it or not."

One of Barn's fingers slid along his crack and then stayed there at his hole, playing, teasing, and then finally pushing in. That was easy, sweet, and he rocked back, humping against that touch.

"Hungry man." God, Barn's gaze was going to burn a hole right through him.

"For you, yeah?" All those pretty men in the club, and Barn was the one for him.

"Yeah, just for me." A second finger pushed into him, Barn sliding both right in deep to find his prostate.

His eyes flew open, knees drawing up.

"Mmm... right there." Just like that another finger pushed in with the first two, stretching and fucking him.

He nodded, throat working, hands reaching for Barney's broad shoulders. "So fucking fine."

Barn smiled at him, working his ass and gland, free hand running over his thighs, his belly. He couldn't stop gasping, couldn't stop his hips from moving.

"You look about ready for more."

"What does that look like?" Go him for making sense.

"That looks like you want more. It looks to me like you were born ready." Those three fingers became four, stretching him wide.

"Barn. Full." His hips arched up off the pillows, toes curling.

"Not as full as you're going to be, babe." Barn grinned down at him, the look half wild, half needy.

He couldn't breathe, couldn't think. He just sort of... begged. Barn fucked him slowly with all four fingers pushing inside him, the promise of that whole fist right there every time Barn's fingers went deep.

"I. Oh." He rolled up, shoulders leaving the bed, eyes feeling like they were burning in his head.

Barn's mouth met his, their teeth clacking with it, the kiss heady, full of want. Craig groaned, almost sobbing into Barney's lips.

While they were kissing Barn's hand disappeared, left him so fucking empty. Then the kiss was gone, too, Barn using more slick on that hand. "Here I come, babe. All for you."

"All... Barney. Barney, please."

"Yeah, babe. Just relax for me now." Barney's free hand rubbed over his belly, stroking the muscles there as fingers pushed against him.

"Talk... talk to me." He couldn't keep his eyes open.

He just groaned, lips parting, gasping as Barney touched him.

"What do you want to hear, Craig?" Barn slowly, but surely, pushed into him, that huge hand stretching him wider and wider. "I could tell you about how you're the sexiest fucking man I've ever seen. You're it for me, babe. Have been since the moment you asked me to come home with you that first time."

"L...love." He couldn't breathe.

"Oh, yeah. Yeah, I love you." The thickest part of Barn's hand spread him, stayed right there for a moment, holding him so open. And then it pushed through, his body closing tight around Barney's wrist.

Craig's cry rang out, body jerking, shuddering.

"Fuck. Just... fuck." Barn watched as his hand moved slowly, carefully. "This always feels like the first time."

"Barney." So fucking full. So full.

"Craig." Barn smiled up at him, eyes glowing for him. *For him.*

"Yeah." He nodded, moaned, no room left for his sound.

Barney's free hand slid around his cock, holding him almost loosely. The other hand... loose was not the right word. Big. Huge. So fucking much. "Holding you in the palms of my hands, babe."

"Yes. Yes, I... Damn. Please." Please.

Both of Barn's hands started moving, sort of counter to each other or something. Craig might have been able to figure it out eventually, except lights were exploding behind his eyes, the sensations utterly blowing his mind. Everything went white-hot and perfect, everything in him screaming.

He could hear Barn's voice, but it was just sound, the words having no meaning. Barn's movements got faster, ratcheting it all up a notch. Craig lost it, coming so hard he couldn't breathe. His orgasm kept going, making him shudder and shake as Barn continued to move, to blow his mind, so fucking huge inside him. He felt like it went on and on, driving him, pushing him higher.

Eventually, it faded away like waves getting farther and farther away from shore, and then Barn's lips were at his ear, murmuring that it was time for Barn's hand to come out.

"I... Love." Craig whimpered, floating.

Barn's lips tickled his earlobes. "I know, babe." A soft hum followed the words, and he almost didn't notice the way Barn's hand stretched him so wide on the way out. He melted into the mattress, limbs too heavy to move.

Barn moved quietly around the room, coming back with a soft, warm cloth, cleaning him up, the come on his stomach, the lube all over his ass. The lights were turned off and then Barney was neck to him, curling around him and tugging him close.

"My Barn." He snuggled in, lips on Barney's jaw.

"Yours and nobody else's, babe." Barn's hand, the hand that had been *inside* him, slid around his hip, holding on nice and tight. "My Craig."

"Yeah."

Yeah.

His.

The bar was looking fucking stunning in the very best tacky and tinselly way, if he did say so himself. Barney grinned into his mug of beer, watching the fairy lights twinkling in the windows. Fairy lights in a bar full of fairies. It tickled him deep inside.

The place was starting to fill up, the Friday night

crowd warming right up to the decorations he and Craig had spent the afternoon putting up.

Of course, he'd spent nearly as much time watching his fine-assed man walking more than a little bow-legged as he had helping decorate. It was Craig's own fault for being such a sexy motherfucker.

Just thinking of his man had his gaze zeroing in. Lean and long, bright red curls shoved back almost brutally, green eyes just shining — his baby was stunning. Studly. Looking well-fucking-fucked.

And wasn't everybody noticing that? The best-looking guy in the place on any given night and all his.

A trio of twinks that he recognized but couldn't put names to came to the bar, looking from him to Craig and back again, laughing and whispering. He just sat a little straighter. That's right, his man was walking funny. His man was fucking fine. Glowing. Smiling. He'd done that. Him.

Barn opened and closed his hand. He could still feel that tight, heated silk around his hand, holding him as much as he was holding Craig. He felt eyes on him, knew Craig was watching him again, staring at him again.

Wanting him again.

He opened and closed his hand once more for effect, and then looked up, met that gaze with his own. He could feel the electricity between them. They were fucking smoldering tonight.

A low chuckle came from next to him and he shot a quick look to find Bob grinning. "You two need to get a room."

"Got one. *Someone* insisted on opening up tonight. You'd think he owned the bar or something." He winked at Bob and went back to checking out the sexiest man in the place.

"Yeah, well. You did good by him. He hasn't looked

so happy in weeks."

"Thanks, man. I like knowing I'm the one who puts the giddy in his up."

"I bet you do." Bob chuckled. "Craig! Buddy! You bringing me another round?"

"I'll have another, too, babe. And one for yourself." They both just wanted to watch Craig walk across the bar again. Barn ate a few beer nuts, his eyes never leaving that bow-legged man of his.

"How's your boy doing?" he asked idly, just to make conversation, trying to remember Bob's lover's name.

"Sweet. Still bruises like a charm."

He chuckled. They all had their little kinks, didn't they? "Good for you, man. Good for you." He licked his lips, watching as Craig came toward them, beers in hand. Look at how fucking careful Craig walked, how it looked so hot, those hips rocking back and forth.

He made sure his hand brushed Craig's as he took his beer, watched with satisfaction as that touch sent a shiver through Craig's body.

"You having a good time, Barn?" Craig was all hoarse from screaming for him. Fuck, that was hot.

"Are you kidding? I get to watch the hottest man in here, knowing I'm going home with him." He sat back and grinned. "I'm having the best time."

"Good. I have to run, man. We're getting busy." Craig leaned down, kissed him good and hard.

He wrapped his hand around Craig's neck, held the kiss a moment longer. "You do what you have to, babe. I'll be sitting and watching and wanting you. Just like every other man here tonight."

"I'm only going home with one, though." Yeah. Yeah, he knew that. He gave his lover something no one else could.

And he planned on giving it to Craig the next three

weeks straight.

Happy Christmas to the both of them.

Hector and Wally
by Julia Talbot

"Hey, Craig. Can I get another one of these?" Hector waggled his nearly empty Coors longneck, feeling the tiny bit of backwash splash around in the bottle.

The bartender turned those powerful green eyes on him, looking him over. "You've had about six, buddy. Maybe you ought to slow down."

Hector growled a little, smacking the bottom of the bottle on the bar. "Damn it, amigo, how am I supposed to drown my sorrows if you won't let me drink?"

"How are you supposed to get home from the middle of nowhere if you drink yourself into a stupor? Have a cup of Joe on me and then we'll see if you want another."

All Hector could do was stare. "You won't take my money?"

"No, sir. Not until you sober up some."

"Goddamn."

Craig grinned and handed him a cup of coffee just the way he liked it, with the dulce de leche creamer. It actually smelled good, and Hector put his drama aside long enough to sip at it.

Nice.

Sighing, Hector took his cup and went to find a booth, the bar getting too crowded to really have a good pout.

"Hey, man, you wanna sit with me?"

Hector glanced over at the guy who'd just waved and smiled, trying to remember his name. He had a nice face, all eye lines and cleft chin, blond hair a little too long... Wayne? Woody? Wally!

"Sure, Wal. How you doing?" Hector sat, his coffee cup cradled in his hands.

"Better than you, looks like. Adrian dump you?"

Lord. Sometimes he forgot how this was the only gay bar in a how-many-mile radius. Everyone knew everyone's business.

"We weren't that close, honey," he said, trying for a sneer. "Let's just say we had a difference of opinion. I didn't want to sleep vicariously with half of Denver."

"Ah. I get that. My last one, Sean? He was that way. Had a revolving door in his bedroom."

Hector only vaguely remembered Sean. Cute little Hispanic guy. "Whatever happened to him, anyway?"

"Huh? Oh, he went to California."

"Where all good Colorado gays go to die, huh?"

"Sheyeah. Asshole." They toasted each other over that one, both of them chuckling. "So, Craig cut you off, huh?"

"He did. Said I'd had enough."

"Well, if you want another one, I can always drive you home."

Huh. Hector thought on that one for a good bit. It was Friday night, so it wasn't like he'd need his car the next day until someone could help him drive out and get it.

"That would rock, man."

"I'll go get us both another."

Wally headed to the bar, and Hector drained his coffee, watching that ass. It was a nice one, as butts went. He approved. By the time Wally got back with two long necks, Hector had made up all sorts of happy little fantasies about that ass.

"Here you go, man."

"Thanks, Wal. You're a prince among queens."

"Ha, ha. So are you trolling for someone new, or just drowning your sorrows?" Those bright blue eyes twinkled at him, telling him Wal was in the market if he was shopping.

"Oh, I think tonight I'm just out for some drama." Hector winked. "I'm not sure I'm ready to plunge back in the pool."

"Well, I'll keep your drama company, then."

It turned out that Wally was good company. Funny, hot, and more than willing to switch to Coke to be the designated driver. By the time he'd had two more beers, Hector was even willing to entertain the idea of jumping back into the dating quagmire. Or at least doing a little humping.

Wally's hand waved in front of his face, drawing him out of some very naughty thoughts. "I hate to ask, man, but it's almost last call. Do you want another, or are you ready to head out?"

"Oh. Oh, we ought to go before everyone gets out to the parking lot, huh?" The whole last call rush was like a herd of water buffalo sometimes. You could sit in the parking lot for an hour afterward.

"Yeah, I was thinking so." Wally stood, stretching a little. "Need to drain the lizard. Be right back."

"Sure." Hector stretched a little himself, feeling off balance and woozy. Damn.

"Hey, man, you're not driving, right?" Bob, the big cop who worked the place clapped him on the back.

"Nope. Wally's got that one."

"Cool. You're looking like you had too many."

"I did. It felt *good.*"

Bob laughed, hand squeezing his shoulder. "Well, just don't let Wally think he's getting anything for a favor you're not willing to give, man."

"No way. I actually like him." Hell, Hector knew he'd been a bit of a slut before Adrian, had a bit of a reputation, but that was all over now. He never wanted to do to a guy what Adrian did to him.

"Cool. Night, man."

"Night." Wally was back, smiling at him and waving at Bob, and they wandered out to the parking lot, the cold January air really making him shiver. "Man, I have nippleage."

"Me too. Mine is the truck down here." An old Chevy sat at the end of the lot, a work truck, all dented up and rusted.

Climbing in, Hector huddled toward Wally, trying to get some warmth as the old heater started up with a blast of cold air. Damn, he hated leaving the bar. That drive home was a bitch.

"So, are you toward Fort Collins or Denver, man?"

"Huh? Oh, Fort Collins. Is that out of your way?"

"Nah. I'm not far from you, I'd bet. Just tell me where to turn."

"Gotcha." Hector settled back once the heater started working, his head bobbing, his eyes heavy and gritty. Damn. Too much beer made for a sleepy Hector.

He woke up a while later with Wally shaking him. "Hey, man, come on. I need directions."

Blinking, he stared out the windshield, trying to get his bearings. Damn. "Uh... We need to turn around and go back one exit."

"No problem."

Luckily, it wasn't. He was close enough to Fort Collins that there were a good many exits. He gave Wally directions, and soon enough he was home, his little rented house bright against Wally's headlights.

"Well, this is the place," he said, trying to find the gumption to reach for the door handle and get out of the truck.

"Cool. You need some help?"

Chuckling, he nodded. "I feel like a pile of goo."

"Lord save us from a man who can't hold his beer." Wally came around and opened Hector's door, helping him out.

He leaned on the guy all the way to the porch. Wally felt good, sturdy and warm, that hard body pressing against his side.

"Nice, man," Hector said, copping a feel.

"Hey, now. Don't start something you're too drunk to finish." Wally turned, face only inches from his, and those well-shaped lips hovered over his, almost touching.

Hector let himself steal a kiss, tasting just a little, needing to touch so bad. Hell, he knew it wasn't gonna happen, and it was probably mean of him, but he just needed a kiss.

Wally kissed him back, hard, all but mashing his lips back against his teeth.

"Shit!" Breaking free, Hector stared at the man, his hand over his mouth, just to make sure everything was still there.

"Sorry. I told you not to tease me, huh?" Wally laughed, but the sound was strained as hell.

"Sorry. Sorry, man, I wasn't trying to tease. I just. I got carried away, huh?" Damn. The man drove him home, got him up to his door, and then Hector did the stupidest thing he could. "Sorry."

"Yeah, yeah. Come on, man. In before you fall down."

Wally chuckled at him, turned him toward the door, the damn thing wavering some.

"I got it." Keys. Where in hell. Ah. There. Keys. He got one in the door, fumbling when it wouldn't turn.

"Oh, good lord. How many keys does a guy need?" Wally propped him up against the side of the house, trying one key after another.

"House. Car. Truck. Uh, mailbox. You know." One of them finally worked, and Hector lurched inside, stumbling to the couch and falling on it.

Someone tugged at his boots, tossed a quilt over him. His keys hit the end table with a clatter. "Better?"

"Yeah. Thanks." His words slurred, and the world started spinning, so he put one foot on the floor. That helped, and he drifted off, murmuring, "Night, Wal."

"Night, honey."

Man, that Wal, he was a sweetheart.

Humming, Hector wandered into Five O'Clock, looking forward to a night of dancing, a few beers, and maybe some pretty boys.

He wasn't in the mood for love, just feeling better than he had in days, maybe in the three weeks since he and Adrian had split. He wanted a longneck and some potato skins, and just to flirt a little, have some fun.

"Hey, man!" Craig waved at him from behind the bar. "How's it hanging?"

"Good. Coors Light, man. How're you?" Craig needed a haircut. Those red curls of his were out of control.

"Doing good. Thinking about buying one of those big screen TVs for the pool room." The longneck slid over, along with a bowl of beer nuts.

"Yeah? That would rock. The flat ones?" People

wondered why he loved this place. It was because Craig was always making it better.

"Yeah. Something cool to watch the games on, you know? Hung up high so no one can fuck with it."

"Yeah. High enough no one will hit it with an errant pool ball, huh?" That would rock.

"Errant pool ball, errant beer bottle, errant fight when some twink asshole gets Isaac all riled up. Pick one." Craig's laugh just rang out, as much a part of the bar as the Tim McGraw Budweiser sign.

"There you go. Hey, Wally!" Hector waved when he saw Wal in the mirror, motioning the man over. "I owe you a beer, buddy."

"Hey, man." He got a grin and a nod, the quiet man propping himself on a barstool. "Bud Lite, Craig. Thanks."

"No prob, Wal. How's things?"

"Work, life, work, work. Same old, same old. You?"

"Ditto."

The cold beer slapped into Wally's hand, the man's callused fingers wrapping around it.

"Long time, no see, man." Hector nudged Wally's ribs. "I'm gonna have some skins. Want a double order?"

"That doesn't sound half bad, man. How's things going? Easing up for you?"

"Yeah. Not bad at all." Wally was a good guy. Asking after him and all. Cute, too. "You doing okay, huh?"

"Working my ass off, just like always." The man was a plumber, he thought, maybe an electrician. Something with houses and emergencies and contractors and money.

"That would be a shame. It's a fine ass." See him. See him wink and flirt.

Wally snorted, laughing right into his beer. "It definitely does its job, connecting my legs to my body."

"There you go." They ordered a double order of potato skins, some cheese sticks and a big quesadilla. "Wanna move to a table?"

"Sure. Craig, man, two more beers?" Wally bought the next round, heading over to plop down next to him.

"Good deal." They sat and chatted. Turned out Wally was a plumber, a good listener, and a hell of a joke teller.

They got to telling bullshit stories — Wally telling him about this woman caught in her hot tub by a bull snake, screaming and carrying on while the water bubbled.

"They look like rattlers, no shit. Had one bite me when I was fishing once, thought I was gonna die."

"No shit? You got a scar?" Wally bent closer to look, grabbing a cheese stick on the way.

"Yeah. Right here." On his damned hand. He'd been reaching for his stringer.

"Goddamn. Did it swell up?" Wally touched the scars, shaking his head.

"Shit, yes. I mean, they ain't poisonous, but it sure tore me up." He'd been a big old baby, too, thinking it was a rattler.

"Bet it scared the living shit out of you. I've been lucky; I mostly get bit by broke pipes and bitchy housewives."

"Housewives, huh? I bet they want to bite you." He'd bite that butt, given half a chance.

"Oh, man. I could tell you some stories. It makes you wonder what all their husbands are up to, or not." Wally's eyes rolled, gimme cap lifted up as he scratched the top of his head. "You kinda want to go, 'Ew. No.'"

"I bet. Sounds kinda like a TV show." Lord, it made him glad he never saw the folks whose houses he worked on.

"I guess." Wally leaned back. "Like one of them Girls Gone Wild things, except with saggy boobs."

"Oh, gross." Shuddering, he sipped at his beer, trying

not to think of saggy titties. "I worked for an old queen one summer during high school who was like that."

"Yeah? Damn." Wally leaned back, legs spread a little. "Well, you ain't got to worry about nothing but the pretty boys on the crew these days, huh?"

"Oh, they're okay. A lot of them would knock my teeth out if they knew I was queer." He winked, shrugging a little.

"Yeah. It ain't like there's a rainbow sticker on my truck."

"So, you figure on a few beers, then we hit the IHOP or something?" That would suit him down to the ground.

"Works for me, man. You want to shoot some pool?"

"You bet. You know Craig's thinking of getting a big screen?" They moved toward the pool tables, snagging the one left empty.

"Yeah? That'd make football season better. We might could tell which team was which."

"No shit. That old set is something sad, huh?" Hector knew he was so gonna get his ass kicked. He wasn't the best pool player in the world.

"It'll do, I guess. Mine's way better at the house." Wally racked up, rolling the balls along the felt. "You want to break?"

"Sure." Yeah, he stood a chance if he could sink one on the break. He'd go for solids.

Wally leaned against the table, stacking up a couple dollars in quarters, just watching.

Taking a deep breath, Hector chalked up and lined up to break, hitting a nice clean shot. He sank one of each, and called solids. Too bad he didn't get his next shot.

Wally sank two, not being bitchy about it, just drinking and bullshitting, keeping the stories coming.

They laughed and drank and by the time someone else wanted the table, they were ready to go get some pancakes. Hell, he couldn't remember having so much fun with anyone in a long time.

Made him wonder why there wasn't someone on Wally's arm and shit, what was wrong with the man, that no one wanted him?

Maybe because he wasn't such a great kisser. Even drunk as a skunk like he'd been, Hector remembered that. "You ready to go, man? I can drive if you need me to."

"I'll follow you." Wally grinned. "I got to be in Aurora at seven in the morning. I'll need my truck."

"Okay, honey. I'll see you at the IHOP." He followed Wal as far as his truck, and damned if he didn't catch himself ogling that ass again, just staring to beat the band. It was a fine thing.

A damn fine thing, actually.

Lord, lord.

The bar was jumping when Hector walked in, and he almost walked right back out. He wasn't sure he was in the mood for that much loud and proud, especially with his head pounding the way it was.

Then he saw Wally at the bar and his headache backed off almost instantly. They'd spent a few long evenings together, drinking beer and munching pancakes. Hector liked the guy a lot, so he wandered on in to say hey.

Wally lifted his beer in greeting, gave him a grin. "Howdy, man. How goes?"

"Hey. I'm tired tonight. Might be a little loud, you know?" He gave Wally a half hug. "Good to see you, though."

"You want to watch the game at my place, man? Craig says there's a big-assed party due in an hour from now."

"Oh, dude. I love your TV." Grinning, Hector nodded. "Let me have one beer, just so Craig doesn't kick me out next time see him."

"Works for me, man." Steve distracted Wally, coming up, slapping the man's back and talking shop.

Hector waved to Craig, got one small draft beer, watching Steve flirt with Wal. Something a lot like jealousy lodged in his gut. Wally laughed and snorted, knocking back that beer. The man turned down another from Steve, though, eyes coming back to look at Hector.

"You ready?" Hector asked, tossing a few more bucks on the bar for Craig. "We can get a six-pack on the way home."

"Sure am." Wally stood up, stretched a little and damn if Steve's eyes weren't on that tight little ass.

Hector stepped between Steve and Wally, real casual-like, reaching out to pat that ass a little. Wally blinked, a soft little moan escaping the man at his touch. Hello. Nice and hard. He didn't ruin the moment by saying anything stupid, just jonesed on the muscled ass and the way Wal was into his touch.

"Come on, man. Looks like the crowd is here." Wally headed toward the door, moving nice and easy, hips swaying, just a little.

"No shit." They passed at least five guys on the way in, some of whom they knew. There was "hi" and "bye" and then he and Wally were out in the cold air and on their way.

Wally drove, heading down the highway to a little subdivision off the road. Wally's house was fucking nice, solid and good-sized, proving that whole thing about plumbers and money.

Plus, he had that great TV.

Hector pulled the beer out and hauled it up to the house, watching that butt all the way. Damn, he was getting fond.

Wally's mutt, Hammy, was dancing, floppy ears flapping as the little son of a bitch bounced.

"Come on in and have a sit, man. I'll let the beast out."

"Thanks." The couch was as nice as the TV. Not new or nothing, but soft and big enough for the both of them.

Wally buzzed around, letting the dog out, grabbing cold beers and putting the six-pack in the fridge.

Hector knew better than to touch another man's remote, so he waited politely for Wal to turn on the TV. "I'm half ashamed to say I don't know what game's on tonight."

"Packers and the Giants. Nothing earth-shattering, especially since that Brett Favre is gone." Wally plopped down, got the TV tuned up.

"Yeah. Sure miss him. Not a bad looking guy, either." Hector winked, kicking off his boots so he wouldn't mess up the couch.

"Hell, no. I wouldn't kick him out of the bed for eating crackers."

Laughing, Hector grabbed the bag of chips Wally had brought out with the beer. "At this point, I'd not kick just about anyone out. Too bad I've gotten picky."

"Yeah? Well, they say that's a good sign. Like self-esteem or some shit." Wally reached over, grabbed a chip and winked at him.

"You think? Maybe it's just that I got someone in mind." He winked back, trying not to come off smarmy.

"Don't tease, now. I'm not on the list, so which hardbody is?"

"Why wouldn't you be on the list?" That ass worth a few bad kisses, for sure.

"I... Am I?" Wally looked fucking shocked.

"Hell, yes. It's nice, 'cause I actually like you." He put his hand on Wally's thigh, not really patting. More petting.

"Well, that's handy, honey. I mean, shit. You're on my list. The whole fucking bar knows it."

He blinked. Well, he'd kind of known that after that first night, but he'd been so drunk and Wally had been so low key...

Wally's cheeks went hot, chin ducking. "Game's fixin' to start, buddy. You want another beer yet?"

"Sure. I'll take another. You want me to get it?" He hoped not. He wanted to watch that ass.

"I don't mind, man." Oh, yeah. Side-to-side, muscles jerking.

Hector thought he might be drooling. Man, he was getting more and more into Wally. He got to watch that ass all the way to the fridge, then Wally bent over. Damn. He couldn't help it. He whistled, a long, loud wolfy sound. That was better than any game.

Wally stood up, stared at him. "You like what you see, man?"

"Shit, yes. You're enough to raise a dead man, Wally." He liked it a lot.

"Well, you ain't dead." Ah, direct and observant.

"No, sir. I'm all alive and sitting here." His cock started to rise against his zipper, letting him know it was ready to go.

He could see Wally's prick filling, swelling in those tight jeans.

Hector pulled Wally down, setting the beer aside, his hands sliding up those lean arms. "You're at the top of the list tonight, I think."

"Yeah?" That cock was right there and he pressed closer, thigh rocking against it.

"Uh-huh. I think you just might be." After his first

experience kissing Wal, he wasn't sure he wanted to ruin the moment trying again, so Hector let his lips move down Wally's neck, licking and kissing.

Wally swallowed, throat working under his lips.

Salty. Hector grinned against Wally's skin. The man tasted just fine. He licked some more, savoring a little.

"Mmm. That's fine." He bit a little and Wally pressed closer, hand wrapping around his hip, tugging.

"It is." Hector moved even closer, until they were pressed so close together you couldn't slide a credit card between them.

Wally's tongue slid over the ridge of his ear, hot and slick and fine. Closing his eyes, Hector threw caution to the wind and turned his head. His lips met Wally's, slow and easy, his tongue darting out to taste.

Oh, that was a sweet, rich sound, Wally humming as the kiss slowly deepened, Wally's tongue sliding against his.

Okay, so one kiss wasn't something to judge by. This wasn't hard and hurty. This was long, rich, and hot. Hector fucking approved.

Things heated up as sweet as you please. Wally knew what to do with those hands, mapping Hector's body, finding one hot spot after another. When they touched his nipples, Hector cried out, his hips rolling. They hardened to a painful degree, but it was fucking delicious.

"Yeah..." Wally eased him back on the sofa, those fingers touching his nipples, almost plucking at them, over and over.

"Shit, Wal!" That was gonna make him come in his jeans, because he'd been idling far longer than he could take, and his body was kicking into high gear.

"This not good for you, honey?" Wally's thumb rubbed the tip of one nipple, soft and easy as you please.

"Oh, fuck. It's good. So damned good." He tried to

remember to touch back, his hands sliding over Wally's chest, down to those lean hips.

He got that ass in hand, thumbs rolling, rocking on the hard, corded muscle, pushing in deep. Jesus fuck, that was a fine ass. Maybe the finest he'd ever held, and they weren't even naked yet. Oh. Naked.

Oh, he could fucking do naked. He got Wally's shirt in his hands, tugged it up out of that waistband. Hot skin appeared, all tanned and pretty, and Hector stroked collarbones and pecs, working down to Wal's flat belly, pulling at the short hairs.

Damn, there was nothing like a man who worked for a living — muscles and scars, hips moving like Wally was going to hump the air.

"Wait for me, honey," he murmured, licking along Wally's shoulder. "I want that skin, too."

"I'll wait. I been waiting for a while..."

"You're a patient man, Wally." Had Wally been watching all this time? It would be hellaciously embarrassing if he'd missed it.

"Works for me, now, too." Damn. Just damn. Fingers cupping Wally's cheek, Hector pulled the man in for another kiss, this one a little harder, a little hotter.

Wally's hips were still rocking, working a little like the man couldn't *not* move.

The kiss was... well, fuck. It was nothing like that first time. Oh, their lips mashed together, and it got desperate, but it was hot. Amazing. Not at all weird.

Wally's hand cupped his cock, fingers working, sliding and rubbing against his balls. Uhn. His head fell back, his hips went up, and it was all he could do not to come. Just like that. Boom. He shook, hanging by a thread.

"I. Skin, man? I want to touch." Wally's fingers found his fly, eased it down nice and slowly, without waiting for him to say boo.

"Hell, yes." Hector figured he'd answer anyway, just to make sure Wally knew he was with the program.

His cock fit in Wally's palm, sliding and slapping against the calluses. Moaning, he pushed harder into that hand, letting Wally give him some friction. Then he got started getting the rest of their clothes.

Wally's jeans were thin enough that they opened up like they had minds of their own. Fucking A. Hector got his hand in, got past the boxer-briefs and got Wally in hand, too. It was good that he was a fast worker, because all of his brain cells went to hell the minute Wally's thumb brushed his slit.

"Fuck. Fuck, man." Wally's eyes rolled, teeth tugging his bottom lip just a little bit.

"Anything you want." He said it against Wal's mouth, his hand moving, working hard.

"You." Wally growled the word out, and then heat shot across his fingers.

Oh. Oh, God, just like that. Just like he'd been worried... Hector yelped, surprised as hell to feel his own come coating his hand, his balls emptying like there was no tomorrow.

"So fine." Wally was grinning like a fool, eyes just laughing for him.

"I didn't know..." What? That Wally would be so damned hot? That he liked being wanted? What?

"That plumbers could fuck? It's a closely guarded professional secret."

"I bet. After all those butt crack jokes." That just tickled him, and Hector started laughing like an idiot, feeling good in his bones.

Wally cackled, big ole hand patting his ass, just like that. "Shit, man. They're just smokescreen."

"I'll remember that. Hell, I'll call you next time I need work done, just so I can watch." That ass. Hector still wanted it, but he was feeling damned lazy.

"Yeah, yeah, yeah. I got drywall needing hung in the workshop. I might could watch that myself." A couple of Kleenex and a tug and a shift and they were settled, both facing the game on the TV, Hector's back pressed to Wally's chest.

Hector relaxed back against the man, head on Wally's shoulder. Fucking paradise. He found his beer, taking a swig. "You know what?"

"What's that, man?"

"I think I just threw away the rest of the list." Wally wasn't just on top. He was the only one there. Who knew?

"Mmm. That works for me, darlin'. It surely does." Wally's rough old fingers petted Hector's belly, just like that.

"Oh, good. Want another beer?" That was settled. They didn't need much more than that, did they? He and Wal, they were just regular guys.

Thank God for that.

The bar was hopping when Hector showed up. Craig was doing some sort of special, he'd bet, but he hadn't been into the Five O'Clock for a while.

Hell, you could say he'd been something of a homebody.

Bellying up to the bar proved to be tough, but Hector elbowed his way in. "Hey, man! Coors Light?"

"Hey, stranger!" Craig was grinning like a fool, sweating a little. "How's it going?"

"Not bad. How's you, man? I haven't been in for a bit." He leaned on the bar, nodding at one of the guys who'd been on the list, once.

The top got popped off, the longneck slid down the bar. "Busy, busy. Lots of boys hunting your ass. You been occupied?"

"I have. Real busy." Just thinking about it made him grin and toast Craig before he took a long drink.

Hell, Wally'd been doing a fabulous job of rocking his fucking world — from sex to cooking to watching stupid ass reality TV.

They'd even been talking about figuring a way to move in together. That blew his mind. Made him take another long drink of beer.

A warm hand wrapped around his hip, Wally's voice calling for a Bud Lite. "Hey, y'all."

"There you are, baby." Grinning, he turned and kissed the corner of Wally's mouth. Why go out in the middle of BF Nowhere to go to a gay bar if you couldn't show off?

"Yup. Got that job finished up, got paid." Wally grinned, kissed him right back. "Got a bonus for hitting deadlines, too."

"Go you, baby. Did you hear that, Craig? Maybe we ought to have a shot, huh?" Tequila was a good look for Wal.

"Mmm. We could have a couple." An envelope was pushed over, his name on the outside.

Hector raised a brow, but didn't ask, just opening the envelope instead. Wal wasn't about games.

In the envelope were two plane tickets to St. Lucia, resort reservations for a week.

Holy shit.

Goddamn. Hector met Wally's eyes, trying not to stare like an idiot. "We're going on vacation?"

"Yep. You and me, honey. Sea and sand and all the sunshine we can bear for a week."

"Oh, man. Yeah." Now he gave Wally a real kiss, a fine hello and howdy and thank you. They drew cat calls.

"Now, now. Y'all break it up. No humping on the bar!" Craig hooted and clapped, sending two beers down the way. "Good news, guys?"

"Hell, yes. Wally's taking me to the beach." As cold as it was in Colorado, he wasn't gonna complain one bit. Wally. Beach. Bathing suits.

"Woo!" They got hoots and hollers, applause, and Wally just kept one arm around his waist, holding on and grinning.

Hector grinned over at his lover, wrapping his own arm around the man tight. "So, does this mean you're moving in with me?"

"No, honey. It means your happy ass is moving in with me. I got a nicer place and room for the dog."

"Oh." Huh. Well, he did have a rental, and Wally owned. "Okay." Hector waited to see what Wally would do with that, watching those pretty eyes.

He got a slow, burning grin, Wally staring at him like he was Christmas and the tree was filled. "We can use your bed, though. It's got a nice bounce to it."

"Lord, lord. Looks like I'm going to have to find a new player for the bar, huh?" Craig was just laughing at them.

"Yessir. This one's taken."

Wally hugged him tight.

"Lock, stock, and barrel," Hector agreed, taking another kiss. He'd been one for playing the field until that Adrian had treated him so bad.

These days, he figured that little shit leaving him was the best thing that ever happened to him.

That and Wally's amazing patience.

The Five O'Clock Bar

Rodeo Man
by BA Tortuga

F uck, rodeo was a sport for the fucking young.
Pistol limped into the bar, the bruises on their third
day, along with the broke ankle and the sprained
fucking wrist that'd keep him out the rest of the season.

"Oh, fuck, man. What *happened*?" Craig looked at
him like no one'd ever seen a broke-dick cowboy before.

"Bronc called Wildfire."

"Oh. Beer?"

"Yeah, with a whiskey chaser." He settled on the
barstool, propped his crutch up. Jesus. He needed to find
someone who'd let him work. God knew he could still
ride.

"Hell of a thing, cowboy," someone said off to his left,
a big old redneck boy settling in on the stool beside him.

"Yeah." Jesus, the man was like a mountain. "She tore
my ass up."

"Looks like it. You know what they say about the
female of the species..." He got a wink, a grin, and bright
green eyes looking him over.

"Yeah, well. I'm getting long in the tooth to straddle

something so big with nothing but a rope."

His beer came, along with his booze, Craig looking wicked as fuck. "And you don't even get lube."

The big guy next to him chuckled, nodding. "Sucks to be dry-fucked, huh?"

"You know it, kid. Shit, I just had enough money to get home and get the electricity turned back on." He did the shot, and then grinned. Man, it was hell to get old.

"So you're a rodeo man, huh?" The guy waved at Craig and another shot appeared.

"Thank you kindly. Yeah, although I'm thinking on giving it up. You?" Oh, fuck, the liquor burned so good.

"Me, what? Oh. No, I don't ride. I mean, I go to rodeos." Lord, the man was all tied at the tongue.

"So what do you do for a living? You got working man's muscles." And a pretty mouth, which you couldn't ever say no more without someone thinking you were weird, 'cause of that movie.

"Oh, I do a little of this, a little of that. Electrical. Plumbing. Fence and shed building." A shrug had all the muscles under that flannel shirt moving.

"Yeah, that's handy as shit. All I got on my résumé is riding fence and throwing myself off broncs."

"There's a lot to be said for that. Freedom in it." Well, hell. Score one for the redneck. He got it.

"No shit, man." He nodded, lifted his beer in salute and they both drank. "You got a name, man?"

The man had bought his skinny ass a shot, after all.

"Dave." One big paw slid his way, calluses showing even more signs of hard work. Proving the guy was older than he'd thought, too.

"Dave." He shook, his hand damn near lost in Dave's.

"Uh-huh. You? Or are you a Dave, too?"

"Pistol. And before you ask, yes, it's really my name.

My daddy was a huge western fan — so we're Pistol, Colt, and Kitty."

"No shit? That had to be hell growing up." The guy sucked down a beer like it was Coke, throat just working.

"More for Kitty than anyone else. It wasn't too bad for me."

"I can see that." He got a sideways look. "Wanna get a pitcher and go sit? You could put that leg up."

"I would." Hell, he could do anything from just sit and visit to imagine eating Mr. Dave up with a spoon.

"Cool. Craig? Can we get a pitcher? You need help man? If not, just leave your glass and hump your ass over to the booth, huh?"

"I got it." He found a real fucking smile, nodding his thanks. Damn, he'd been out of good company too long if a simple kindness made him grin. He clumped over to the table, groaning when he eased his leg up and, in seconds, Dave was sliding into the seat across from him, smiling and pouring him a fresh beer.

"Man, you are a champ." His fucking ankle was throbbing like a motherfucker. "Thanks."

"No problem. I been there. Fell off a roof once, working on gutters. Broke my leg in two places." Dave winked, elbows on the table.

"Oh, damn. That's got to be a bitch." It happened so fast with the broncs that you forgot to hurt for a minute.

"It is. Never worked up there without a wire again."

Somehow the image of Dave's big old body dangling from a wire and harness, swinging like a flying trapeze, just tickled him. He chuckled. "Where do they hook the wire up to?"

"We stick a doolie under the shingles. Then we pull it out." Dave grinned. "I don't work roofs much no more."

"That's pretty cool." Pistol poured another glass, leaning back. "Man, it's nice to be home, somehow."

"Been on the road awhile, huh?" They had a bowl of peanuts, and they started working through them. Salty goodness.

"God, yeah. I made the finals last year, but this season? Man, it's kicked my butt."

"And your leg." Winking, Dave stretched, muscles bulging. Nice.

"Leg. Wrist. You name it, it's been kicked."

"Ow. So, how long are you looking at for it to heal?"

"Six weeks, give or take." Pistol shrugged. "I can still ride and stuff, so I'll hunt work."

"Yeah? Well, let me know if you don't find anything that suits you." Dave pulled out a card that had "Dave's Handyman Service" printed on it.

"Oh, man. You are a broke-dick cowboy's wet dream. I mean it." And he didn't just mean the whole job part.

"I can live with that." Look at Dave's eyes shine. "I surely can."

Pistol's prick went hard in a sudden rush, making his Wranglers tight. Oh, man. He vaguely remembered how to flirt. Sort of. He let himself look, eyes dragging up and down. "Yeah."

Dave cleared his throat. "This is where I'd normally play footsie, but I don't want to hurt you."

Pistol grinned, nodded. "Well, we can use our left feet, if you want."

"Oh, there you go." Sure enough, a big old foot slid alongside his, gentle as you please.

"Oh, that works." Damn, he could play on that body like a jungle gym.

"Good." A wealth of satisfaction sounded in that voice. The toe of Dave's boot slid up his leg.

Pistol caught himself spreading, sliding down a little.

"Uh-huh."

Oh, hell yeah.

"So, what do you do when you're not bucking or working, Pistol?" Wait? The man expected him to think with the sole of that boot almost at his balls?

"I haven't... uhn... I haven't figured that out yet, darlin', but I got me some ideas."

"No, no. I mean what do you like? Blow 'em up movies? Line dancing? Pin the tail on the old stud?" That was just wicked.

"I like to play cards, dominoes. I got a little TV in my trailer, too. Got some movies."

"I like movies, myself, and I love gin rummy."

"Yeah? I haven't played that in a long time."

"Maybe we could get together sometime and play, huh?" Dave was wanting to play something, for sure. Pistol could see it in those bright eyes.

"I got some free time these days, I do." Pistol shifted, pressed against that foot a little, his balls aching.

Dave moaned a little, pupils dilating. "Yeah? Your leg doesn't, uh, impede you?"

"It's my ankle. That's way, way south of the border."

"Well, then. If you wanna play some cards tonight, you just let me know." His balls pulled right up under the full pressure of Dave's foot.

"Your deck or mine, honey?" God knew his momma didn't raise no shrinking violet.

"Yours. You'll be more comfortable there, yeah? I know it sucks to not be able to find the bathroom." The man was almost too good to be true. God knew Pistol hoped that didn't mean Dave had someone else at home.

"Works for me. I've got a little trailer house. Nothing fancy, but not trashy neither."

"I have a messy one bedroom condo. It's a wreck." Dave gave him a shrewd look. "Not hiding anyone there, though."

"No? Cool. I'm not into that, you know? I mean, there's something to be said for honesty."

"Yeah. I'm not a player, man. What you see is what you get." Dave stretched again and drained the last of his beer. "You about ready?"

"I am." Pistol stood up, swaying a little, the beer and booze going to his head.

"Hey. Hey, you okay?" Dave hopped up and caught his arm, holding him steady.

"Yeah. Just haven't had a lot to eat." He took a deep breath, the oxygen steadying him.

"We can get something on the way to yours." Dave held on until Pistol felt like he could do this thing.

"Sure. You driving, man?" He could spring for KFC.

"You got it." Hell, Dave even slid an arm around his waist so he didn't have to use crutches. Someone's momma raised him right.

They got out of the Clock okay, the guys waving and laughing, and headed out into the wind, the parking lot dark as pitch. "Damn. Craig needs to put lights out here."

Of course, they all knew why Craig didn't.

"Yeah, well, I can find my truck in the dark." Dave patted Pistol's ass, almost making him fall over.

His arm wrapped around Dave's heavy waist, his hand sliding over Dave's hip.

"Mmm. Cowboy hands. Where's your ride? Just so we both remember in the morning." Dave got him settled in the truck, looking around the lot once the engine was going and the lights were on.

"See the big red Ford with the one blue door? She's mine." Dave's truck was nice, if dusty as all get out.

"Cool." The big truck roared and they headed out. "Just tell me which way, man."

"It's just down the highway here. Happy Acres." Of all the bullshit-named places, this one was the best for the money. Hell, the water worked most of the time.

"Cool."

They listened to George on the way, pretty much just not talking, but it wasn't uncomfortable at all. It was nice. He pointed when they came up to the exit, the trailer park right there, his little place located three rows back.

Dave parked, the lights clicking off, the engine and radio going silent. They sat there for a minute before Dave gave him a grin. "You okay?"

"Yeah. Yeah, man. I might be better than okay." He hadn't picked someone up and brought them home in a long damned time. Of course, he had the sneaking suspicion *he'd* gotten picked up instead.

"Come show me your place." That big body moved like a shifting mountain, Dave getting out of the truck and coming around to help him down.

Pistol slid down that solid mass of muscle, his boot dangling a second before it touched the ground. "Come on in, honey."

The place was simple as hell, but clean enough — TV and futon and stereo and little kitchen table.

"Looks comfy." Those big hands stayed on him, helping him to the couch, lowering him down. "You want me to grab us a drink?"

"Surely. There's Cokes, beer, and bottled water in the fridge."

"What do you want?" He got a view of a tight ass, wider than a cowboy butt, but still nice and hard and round, when Dave went to the fridge.

"Water, I think." He wasn't in the mood to miss anything he and Dave might get up to.

"Mind if I have a Coke?" Things bumped and shifted in the fridge before Dave came back, handing him a bottle of water.

He scooted over, giving Dave room. "Thanks. Have a seat." Have a cowboy.

Easing down next to him, Dave patted his leg. "Looking good."

"Shit, man. You make an old cowpoke feel damn good."

"That's the idea. We need to both feel good, huh?" Looked like the preliminaries were over, because Dave leaned right over and kissed him. Pistol let the unopened water bottle fall, his hand sliding right on up that strong, muscled arm. The Coke can clumped down on the coffee table, Dave turning just a bit to slide closer, hand falling to the inside of Pistol's thigh.

Oh, fuck, yes.

Pistol slid closer and twisted a little, cock rubbing against whatever he could reach.

"Hungry man." Chuckling, Dave undid Pistol's zipper, pulling his jeans and briefs out to the way to touch him.

"Oh, damn. You know it, honey. You're a feast." He rippled, pushed right into the touch. Oh, damn. Hot.

"You think? I tell you what, most guys think I'm a little thick." Yeah, he knew how persnickety gay guys could be.

"Honey, I could eat you up." He had a thing for big guys, solid men. Working men.

"Well, come on." The hand not on his prick cupped the back of his head, pulling him in for a kiss. Dave had a hot mouth and a heavy, needy kiss. It was worth spending time on, and the kiss went on and on, both of them groaning, tongues sliding against each other's.

"Do you... I mean, is there somewhere we can get you more flat?" He got a grin, those bright eyes twinkling for him, Dave's cheeks hot.

"Uh-huh. I got a bed. Takes up the whole room."

"No shit? I could see that." Levering up, Dave held down a hand. "Come on, honey. Let's get comfy."

He reached up, hand slapping into Dave's. They hauled him up together, their chests bumping. Dave gave him another kiss, just for good measure, probably. It felt even better, because he got to lean all his weight on that big body and feel up all those muscles. From the solid belly to that chest like a bull, Pistol was all the fuck over it.

"Mmm. Man, you have a good mouth, Pistol." Half carrying, half dragging, Dave took him to the bedroom, getting him down on the bed and skinning his jeans down his legs.

Pistol had never felt so much like he was wanted. Damn.

The big man knew just how to touch him, just how to get him laid out so they could get busy. Yeah. Hot. Those hands slid over his skin, rough as cobs, but all the sweeter for it. Together they managed to get both of them naked, and goddamn, look at that skin. He could ride and ride. He slid his hands down Dave's belly, tugging at the little hairs.

"Oh. Yeah." Kneeling on the bed next to him, Dave stroked his chest, thumbs rubbing his nipples.

His hand wrapped around Dave's cock, measuring from base to tip, twisting his hand, tugging right at the tip. Nice. Hot, long and thick, Dave filled his hand, and Pistol could count the man's heartbeat. He rolled, getting closer, watching his hand move on that fat shaft.

Dave grunted, humping his hand, staring right into his eyes. Damn. Leaning down and down, Pistol finally got his lips around the tip of Dave's cock, tongue sliding over the slit.

"Oh. Oh, God, honey. That's... I could do for you, too."

Yeah. Dave could taste him, too.

"Uhn. Yes. Fuck, yes." He nodded, letting his mouth drop a little farther. Dave shifted just a bit, turning, moving, mouth sliding down his belly. When the tip of Dave's tongue touched the head of his cock, he thought he might just explode.

It was easy to let Dave see how good it felt by humming around Dave's cock, his tongue sliding around the tip. Dave moaned for him, taking him in deep, hands holding his hips, giving him leverage. He forgot all about his damned ankle, just sucking and humping.

Pistol closed his eyes, taking as much as he could, hands wrapped around the shaft that was left.

Their skin heated up, their hips started circling, both of them searching for more. One big finger slid back behind Pistol's balls, sending sparks up and down his spine. He swallowed hard, sucking until his saw sparkles behind his eyelids. Fuck, yeah. More.

They moved together, both of them sucking, both of them hard enough to pound nails. He could feel Dave's balls drawing up against his hand, against the base of that fine cock.

Damn.

Just, damn.

Pistol's toes curled, and he had to focus on not fucking this up, not biting because he needed to. Dave took him all the way down, sucking at the base of his cock, and suddenly he wasn't worrying about anything. He was flying.

He came so hard that his bones rattled, his mouth going lax for a minute.

Dave stilled, waiting for him to catch up before thrusting again. As soon as he closed his lips, Dave gave one, two more thrusts, and then came for him, giving him all that salty, bitter heat.

"Oh. Oh, damn, honey." Pistol groaned, tongue

cleaning that heavy cock off before he leaned back.

"Mmm. God, yeah. You're hotter than a..." Dave laughed, the sound vibrating against his leg. "I bet you get that a lot."

"Less often than you'd imagine."

"I can imagine all sorts of things, man, but I'd just as soon not think of you with a bunch of other guys." He got a pat, a wink, and a kiss.

He chuckled, grinned. "Not my thing. I'm more about the focusing on what's in hand."

Pistol squeezed Dave a little, proving his point.

"I can get behind that. You comfy, man? Don't want to squash you." That big body shifted against his, settling more along his side.

"I'm happy." He was, too. Weird, given that he'd been in one hell of a mood.

"Good." Yeah, there was a wealth of satisfaction in that one word. "Gonna nap now."

"Uh-huh." He patted Dave's belly and snuggled in. Naps worked.

Dave bellied up to the bar, smiling at Craig. "Hey, man. How's it going?"

"Good!" Craig was boogying, red head bopping to the beat of an old western swing song. "Where's your Siamese twin?"

"Ha ha." He and Pistol weren't attached at the hip, even if they had been seeing a lot of each other. Dave did love him a cowboy. "He had to get his ankle checked out and went home to sleep it off." That shit hurt.

"Bummer, man. Beer?"

"Yeah."

Turning on his stool, Dave surveyed the bar. It wasn't

exactly jumping tonight, and Dave knew he wouldn't be there himself if Pistol had been up for a movie and McDonalds or something.

"So what are you going to do when he goes back to rodeo'in?"

"Huh?" He tilted his head back to look at Craig.

"Pistol. He'll go right back to the game once he's healed up. Rodeo men don't stay."

Yeah. Well. Dave knew that. Knew it, and didn't care. Any time he could spend with the man would be worth it. 'Course, hearing it from Craig didn't help. Made the night a little less shiny.

Shaking his head, Dave pushed a five across the bar and drained his beer. "Thanks, man. Thought bartenders were supposed to cheer people up."

He headed out, glad-handing a few old buddies who said they were missing him these days, avoiding the little meat market boys.

Dave didn't really want to go home, so he stopped at the Mini Mart and got some gas before heading on up Twenty Five, letting the wheels spin. He'd done some long-haul trucking once upon a time, and had found that he did his best thinking listening to the thump of rubber on the highway.

The headlights lit the way almost all the way to Cheyenne before Dave pulled off and stopped at an all-night pancake place, a little buffet set up and a pretty-as-a-button little Asian waitress making him smile as he settled in for some serious midnight breakfast.

"Lonely?" the waitress asked him when she brought his third cup of coffee, and he did a double-take, figuring there was no way she was hitting on him. She had a wedding ring on, anyway.

Nodding, he held out his cup. "Yeah, honey. Missing someone, which is kinda stupid."

"Ah." She smiled, all sympathy. "Is hard, not being together, huh?"

"Oh, we've been together. I'm just worried that he'll..."

"He'll what? Cheat on you?"

Man, he'd been worried there for a minute about blurting out that he was gay. She didn't bat an eye. "Nah. I know he wouldn't cheat. He's a rodeo guy, though."

"Ah," she said again, nodding sagely. "You afraid he'll run off."

"Pretty much, yeah."

"Then why are you here? You should be with him. Spend as much time as you can while you can." She winked and flounced off, her little apron butt shaking.

Maybe she had been coming on to him. Who knew?

He ate his way through two plates of pancakes before he pulled out his cell phone. He flipped it open and dialed Pistol's number.

"Hey, man," he said when Pistol picked up. "How you feeling? A little queasy, huh? Look, I was thinking, I could bring you a milkshake and maybe a sandwich. Yeah? Cool. I can be there in about an hour."

He hung up and smiled. Yeah. Spend the time when you can. That was his new motto.

Pistol leaned on the bar, laughing a little at the story that Crazy Tim was telling him. Lord, he did love that insane son of a bitch. They'd ridden the circuit together since he was a sixteen-year-old asshole lying about his age and hitching rides to wherever he could get to.

Crazy'd been the one who picked him up after that first event where he couldn't get back up on his own, plopped his scared ass in an old Ford and headed toward

Laramie, a streak of clown makeup on one cheekbone. From that day on, Crazy'd been his hero, his best friend, his big brother.

He shouldn't have been surprised to see the weird eyes appear at his door — one sky blue, one black as pitch. "Howdy, son! I missed you. Buy me a beer!"

Now they were on beer number three, both laughing their asses off as Crazy told him about Joe Michael and how that cowboy'd taken a bet to ride Mayo back-asswards, holding onto the flank strap for all he was after the contractors had all gone off to bed.

"...and I swear to you, son. That stupid fucker was bouncing around like the last popcorn kernel in an oiled pan. Then Mayo sets to spinning like he never would during the eight and bam! Joey goes ass over teakettle, lands flat on his back in the dirt. You could see them little birdies, flying around his head going, 'chirp, chirp, chirp.'"

Pistol hooted, slapping his leg. "Lord, that boy ain't got the good sense God gave a goat."

"Nope, but I tell you what, that damn Mayo? He's been good for two eighty-pointers and a ninety one."

He blinked. Hell. He'd never seen that bull buck worth a shit. "No shit?"

"Swear to God."

"Well, I'll be damned."

Crazy nodded happily, looking pleased as shit to be able to share some news that he hadn't heard. "Things on the bronc end are going about the same as always. Hondo got himself a little gal pregnant, Bonner's riding good, Dan's broke his nose in a bar fight, but he's riding. Did I tell you that the Redding twins lost their daddy? Heart attack. Real sudden, but there weren't no pain, they said."

He winced and murmured, asking after Missus Redding

like he was 'sposed to, but otherwise just enjoying the hell out of himself.

A hand landed on his shoulder, patting real quick. "Hey, Cowboy. I got your message."

He couldn't have stopped his grin if he wanted to, which he so didn't. "Dave! I got an old friend I want you to meet. Dave, this is Crazy Tim Martin. Crazy, this is Dave. He's..."

Crazy chuckled, stood to shake Dave's hand, coming about up to his big lover's bellybutton. "Hell, if he's making you grin like a fool, I reckon I know what he is to you. Pleased."

Dave chuckled and shook, nodded. "I imagine you're right. I've heard a lot about you."

"And it's all good, I know. Have a seat, son, and I'll buy the next round." Crazy motioned to Craig, just grinning ear-to-ear. "So, Dave, you ever thought about steer wrestling? You're a big boy; you'd do just fine at it."

Pistol grinned over at Dave, happy as a pig in shit, their knees resting together.

Dave was jonesing on the whole Pistol situation.

They'd seen each other three or four times in the last few weeks, and Pistol had picked up some odd jobs from him. The man seemed to like Dave for who he was, and God knew Pistol was a fan of Dave's form. It made for some damned hot nights.

Tonight, they were heading into Aurora to have steak at Emil-Lene's, this great little steakhouse that had the biggest pepper grinder ever, and damned fine relish trays. Then they'd hit the Five O'Clock for drinks. Then who knew what?

Dave hit Pistol's trailer at five-thirty, the Old Spice smell finally starting to die down a little.

That tanned-leather face appeared, grin reaching from ear to ear. Oh. Oh, damn. Starched jeans, crisp white shirt, good watch and dress boots, even the 5X hat. He ranked up there.

"Hey, darlin'. Come on in."

"Hey." He stepped in, taking off his gimme cap so he could bend for a kiss without putting Pistol's eye out. "How's you?"

"Getting better all the time." That short, lean body stretched all up against him, feeling damn good.

"Yeah?" He started grinning and just couldn't stop, his arms coming up to hold Pistol close. "Cool."

"Uh-huh. You smell good." That tiny cowboy ass fit perfectly in his hands.

"Just Old Spice." A shower. A new shirt. He had it bad.

"Mmmhmm. Just right." Those square hands slid down his belly, solid as could be.

"We don't want to be late for supper," he warned, trying to ignore how hard he was getting.

"Nope. We don't." His cock got cupped, fingers rubbing a little. "And you promised steak."

"I did." If he squeaked a bit, Dave figured he was entitled. Hell, he went up on his tippy-toes for that.

"This'll keep us nice and warmed up for that then." He got himself another kiss, deep and long and hot enough to curl his short hairs.

"Uh-huh." Warm. More like nuclear hot. Dave steered Pistol toward the door. "Come on, cowboy. Steak. Weird spaghetti. Pickles."

"I like pickles." Pistol was walking good now, barely limping at all.

"Did I know that?" He probably had. He thought

maybe Pistol liked them fried.

"Prob'ly. We had them the other day somewhere." Look at that ass, swaying back and forth.

"Uh-huh. At that brew pub." They headed on out, and he kinda missed having to help Pistol into the truck.

Pistol grinned at him, hopping up, that cowboy hat put on the hook in the back.

The radio had Alan Jackson on, and Dave bellowed along, pounding the steering wheel with his fingers. Pistol just laughed at him.

"Sing it, baby!" They headed down the highway, bouncing and goofing off.

The parking lot with the big tree appeared at the end of their headlights, and Dave coasted down the little hill, the smell of steak strong.

"Oh, man. That's heaven on a grill." They parked by the little white building, next to all of the other pickups. "Looks like our type of place."

"It does. We got us a reservation and everything." The old lady that met them at the door looked like she was older than the cowboy-themed prints hanging on the wall, but she was a sweetheart.

"Good evenin', ma'am." Pistol nodded, tipped his hat, looking about at home as he could be.

"Hello, son. Want to hang your hat?" She showed them to their table, her painted, sagging face lighting up in a smile. Pistol lived up to his name. Everyone thought he was a hoot on sight.

"Yes, ma'am. This place is just wonderful. Smells like the best place on Earth."

She winked. "It is."

They got settled and got their order in, which was an effort in and of itself as there was no menu. The waitress just rattled off specials. It was fucking worth it, though, to see Pistol moan over that steak.

And the pickles.

He got to see Pistol's laughter over the pepper mill, too — the damn thing was so big Pistol had to hold the bottom, the waitress using both hands to spin it. When the lady came to ask if they wanted dessert and coffee, they were stuffed to the gills and ready for a beer. "I think we'll pass, honey. It was amazing."

"It was. Y'all should be proud." Pistol looked like a python that had swallowed a goat, the way his belly was pooching out.

"Thanks, boys." The old lady took their check, and they rolled their big old bellies out of the restaurant.

"Damn, honey. That was *fine*. Thank you." Pistol looked almost well-fucked, all lazy and sated.

He patted that tight ass. "It was. I like having a steak with you, man."

"Shit, honey. There hasn't been much you and me've done that hasn't been top-notch." That was the truth. Hell, Pistol liked just sitting with him and eating popcorn.

"Yeah... You want to skip the bar?" He'd love to just go home and watch a movie.

"Sure. We could just take it easy on the sofa."

"That works for me. We could have an action adventure night." His hand landed on Pistol's thigh after he got into the truck.

"Sounds good." Pistol spread, just a little, letting him touch.

"Mmm." His turn to tease a little. Dave let his fingers press the seam of Pistol's jeans.

"Damn, I do love your hands, honey." Pistol rippled, rocking up toward his fingers.

"I like them on you." Lord, he was happy. It hit him, really, right then, how good life was.

"Fucking A." Pistol leaned toward him, smiling. "I tell you what, honey. I've never been so happy to be home."

He gave Pistol a kiss. "Good. I hate that you had to crack yourself up to do it, but I'm glad we met."

"You know it. Now take me home with you and I'll seduce you on the sofa, suck you off while the DVD player runs."

"Oh. Oh, God. Yes, please." How on earth was he going to drive now?

Pistol leaned closer, whispering in his ear. "You know how I feel about that — your fine fucking body."

"I do." He turned his face just a little and took a kiss, letting his tongue slide out to taste. Beautiful man.

He couldn't wait to get home.

The Five O'Clock Bar

Trouble Left Him
by Chris Owen

The Five O'Clock hadn't been open for any more than half an hour when trouble walked in, looking faintly disgusted and a bit pissed off. He also looked exactly like a prissy, snobby, overly-done-up, bleached and waxed wanna-be fashion model, and he brought with him a cowboy who had to be just plain stupid to be seen with such a toy.

The pretty little boys didn't tend to show up this early in the day, preferring instead to hold court at night even if they were egged on by their sugar daddies like this cowboy. Kyle sat up and took note as the sneering kid stepped into the bar, squinting as the angle of the sunset threw one last beam right up into his eye. Probably served him right.

From where he sat at the edge of the bar, Kyle had a great view. He raised his eyebrow at Craig, who kept on polishing a glass without giving the two newcomers more than a glance and a friendly hello. Craig was like that; he didn't judge anyone unless they were causing trouble in his bar, and these two weren't. Yet. They came right up to the bar, the kid looking sulky and the cowboy looking as pleased as could be.

With one hand on the pretty dolly's back, the cowboy nodded, his hat brim dipping low, and grinned right at Craig. He rumbled, low and smooth, "You order a drink, baby. I'll be right back." He didn't wait for a reply, but took a fast look around and headed to the bathrooms.

"Yeah, sure, Chet. I'll do that." The kid, who actually looked a lot older close up, didn't sound overly pleased.

Cowboy Chet either didn't care or didn't notice. He walked past Kyle, still grinning happily, and tipped his hat again. Kyle had to assume he hadn't heard. The man was too damn cheerful to let his boyfriend's attitude ride.

Kyle smiled right back at him, liking the guy's eyes even if he did have lousy taste in men. Kyle checked out the view from the other side, too, not caring if the whiny half of the pair saw him or not. If it came to it, Kyle knew he could take out the kid with one solid punch.

Cowboy Chet had a stellar ass, all dressed up in nice, tight Wranglers.

Kyle looked back up, fully prepared to give Chet's pal a defiant glare, but the kid wasn't paying any attention. He was looking at Craig, his mouth set into a thin line.

"What can I get you?" Craig asked with a friendly smile.

"He'd like to have a shot and a beer, probably, and I doubt you even know how to make what I drink. Can I just have a pen?"

Craig's eyebrows shot up. Kyle set his beer down, nice and easy. Wordlessly, Craig passed over a pen from the cup by the register.

Without even a "thank you," the kid pulled out his wallet and took a card from it. He scribbled a couple of lines on the back and set it on the bar, then handed Craig back his pen. "Thanks," he finally said. He didn't sound like he meant it.

"No problem." Craig took the pen and tossed it toward the cash register. "You want anything else?"

"Nope." The asshole moved away from the bar and shook his head. "Not one damn thing." And then he left, rushing out the door like his tail was on fire.

"Well." Craig watched him go. "I guess he doesn't want a drink."

Kyle snorted and came around the edge of the bar to look at the card. "Not like we need his kind in here anyway." He picked up the card and read it. "Oh, ouch."

"That bad?" Craig leaned over and took the card, then winced. "I think I'll just—" He broke off as Cowboy Chet swaggered back out.

There was a pause and Kyle debated for a moment, that nice *calm* moment before the shit hit the fan. He wondered if he could possibly get back to his spot at the end of the bar and make it look natural, or if he should man up and stay where he was. He wasn't worried about himself, or getting in the way of Chet's anger, but more concerned for the man's pride. It had to suck to be left like that. It would suck more to know there were witnesses.

As the moment ended, however, Kyle realized there was no way he was going to be able to just slide away, so he held his ground. One hip pressed into the bar, one hand around his beer. He wished he had his hat on, but he'd hung it up like his mother had raised him to do inside.

"Excuse me." Chet had a nice voice, and he was being polite. Given that he was also looking around the bar like he'd misplaced something important, that was saying a pretty good thing, Kyle thought. "I came in here with a blond fella, about this high. Don't suppose you know where he went?"

Craig sighed and started pulling a beer, one hand

rubbing the top of the tap. "Yeah," he admitted, sliding the beer across the bar to Chet. "He left you a note." Craig shoved the card next to the glass. "Shot coming up." His look was full of sympathy and Kyle lifted his chin, asking for a shot, too. Misery often liked to have a drinking partner.

Chet looked baffled for a moment. "A note?" He picked up the card and read it, one foot lifting to rest on the bottom rung of a barstool.

Kyle looked away. There were limits, after all, and Craig was lining up glasses. That could be fascinating to watch, if Kyle tried hard.

"Well, don't that beat all." Chet tossed the card back onto the bar and reached for the beer. "Thanks, friend."

"On the house." Craig poured out the shot and gave Kyle a piercing look, then grinned. "You, too. But only because I know you're going to behave yourself."

"Yes, Craig," Kyle said dutifully. "Kind of you."

Chet pulled the bar stool out with his foot and put himself down on it. "Kind of you," he echoed. The hat came off, the shot went back, and his throat worked, swallowing it down. "And I'll take another, please."

"You got it." Craig poured again and then headed down the bar to have a word with a guy who'd just come in from the other room.

Chet flipped the card over so the words were face up. *Had enough of this crap. Going home.* He swallowed his second shot and took a long pull off his beer, then sighed. "You know," he said slowly, carefully. "The bitch of it is, my phone was in the car."

Kyle sat himself down next to Chet and drank his own shot. "Maybe you can get it back. Note says he's going home, so you know where he is, right?"

Chet flipped the card again, printed side up. The card now read *Chester Willows, Custom Woodwork, Custom*

Designs and had a Colorado address. "Home for him is California. He's long gone."

Kyle drank his beer and looked at Chester Willows out of the corner of his eye. He guessed Chet was maybe a couple years older than himself, easing up on forty. He had lines around his eyes that sure looked fine when the man smiled. He had a cleft in his chin and high, sharp cheekbones, along with a dash of gray in his hair. His hands were marked up and he acted like a cowboy even if he was in woodworking and design, whatever the hell that meant.

"Don't take this the wrong way," Kyle said slowly, looking away from Chet and into his beer. "But he really don't seem like your type. More... fancied up. Not real."

Chet grinned and gave him a fast look, those lines at the corners of his eyes turning into crinkles. "I'm not all broken up about it." He offered Kyle his hand. "Chet Willows. Sorry you had to see me at my least graceful."

"Kyle Banks." Kyle shook his hand and held on a wee bit too long, purely by accident. "I thought you were full of grace. You didn't even swear."

"I don't, much, unless I cut myself." Chet drank from his beer and then set it aside like he was going to save the rest. "That was Ricky James DeLong of Redding, California. He likes to think he's a surfer."

Kyle thought for a moment. "Redding is kind of far from the water."

"Exactly. Ricky James wasn't much like he said he was."

"So why the hell were you with him?" Kyle wanted to bite his tongue as soon as the words were out. He didn't know shit. It might have been a long-term thing, or Chet and Ricky James might have met that morning. Plus, it wasn't exactly his business, since he'd known Chet for all of three minutes himself.

Chet's eyes crinkled right up and he picked up his beer again. "Well, now." His cheeks grew a tiny bit pink as he leaned closer to Kyle. "There wasn't nothing I could think of that that boy wouldn't do and he taught me a few tricks, too. Best sex of my life, really. I did more weird shit in the last six months than in the rest of my life all together."

Kyle tried not to choke on his beer. "I— God, what am I supposed to say to that? 'Weird shit'?"

"Uh-huh." Chet's cheeks were getting damn near red now. "Ricky James, he was all show and bang, not a lot of depth, and he thought he'd come in and show me a thing or two, teach me to be all presentable. He liked having a cowboy of his own, see? And I liked having a good time for a change. He'd let me do things like hold him down and tie him up, gag him. But he wasn't shy about demanding stuff either, and some of the things he wanted were kinkier than I thought I'd be into. I think that's when he started getting bored."

"Craig, 'nother shot, please." Kyle thought his voice might have been a bit thick.

"You got it. Just because I'm nosy, can you tell me who's driving?" Craig asked as he set them up again. "I'll be taking your keys, I think."

Kyle passed them over without a word. "We'll be takin' a cab." Kyle tossed back his drink and made sure he was facing dead ahead, his hips fronting the bar. No need to let his new friend know that he'd be jerking off half the night thinking about him.

Craig kind of smirked at him as he poured and set up another set of shots and more beer, too. "I do like that 'we,' Kyle," he said just for Kyle to hear. "It's about time, even if it is just a stop over."

Kyle rolled his eyes, drank, and went back to looking at Chet.

Chet drank, too, and went on talking. "So, Ricky James got bored and as he was the one with the car and I was the one with the money, he had a bit of freedom to walk, I guess. I'd only filled the tank an hour ago. I'm just glad we made it back into the right state."

"Road tripping?" Kyle figured he better stick to short sentences until his cock went back down. He was stuck on thoughts of Chet holding him down. He'd let Chet do that, hell, yes. Well, assuming Chet earned it, of course.

"Five months, twenty states. It's been a long time since I've seen home." Chet looked thoughtful for a moment. "First thing I'm going to do when I manage to get my ass home is buy a horse. God, I miss riding."

Kyle blinked at him. "You haven't been on a horse in five months?"

"Nope." Chet looked downright embarrassed. "Too busy being stupid, I guess. At least I didn't fall in love with him." He finished his beer in a series of swallows. "Time to get back to real life. Good riddance and all that."

Kyle nodded and toasted Chet with the beer at his hand, not sure if it was his or he had a new one or if he'd just stolen someone else's. He didn't care. "To real life!"

Chet beamed at him and toasted back with a shot glass. "Next stop, the nearest horse barn."

"I got one of those." Kyle nodded when Chet beamed at him. "I do. Wanna go see?"

"Oh, boy." Craig cleared up the empty glasses around them. "It's not even past supper time, Kyle. You wanting that cab already?"

Chet pulled out his wallet and started giving Craig bills. "We're gonna go see Kyle's horse."

"Man's got nine or ten." Craig took the money and counted some out, then shoved the rest back at Chet. "I'll get you boys out there — I'll call a cab right now. And who knows — there's still time for y'all to sober up and come on back." He passed Kyle his hat with a flourish.

"Maybe." Chet put his hat back on and finished whatever glass was left. Kyle had lost track. "We'll just have to see what happens."

"Oh, I got a pretty good idea." Craig winked at Kyle and walked away, leaving him blushing.

A few minutes later, safely piled into the back of Tubby Stebbins' cab, Kyle thought maybe Craig was right. Tubby was looking so far the other way that Kyle wondered how the man was driving, and Chet had one hand high up on Kyle's thigh. He wasn't exactly groping, and he was talking animatedly instead of kissing, but a man would have to be blind to miss the way Chet and Kyle were reacting to each other.

Tubby, thankfully, wasn't blind. It made him a great cab driver, even if it did make for awkward social situations.

Chet told Kyle all about the places he'd seen and the rodeos he gone to, and the car Ricky James had seen fit to take on the road — a big old gas guzzling Ford soft-top — and by the time Tubby dropped them off at Kyle's, they'd moved on to discussing horses and bulls.

The buzz had backed off to where another beer seemed like a fine idea to Kyle. The sun was long down but his horses knew their land and there were three or four Kyle would trust to carry him around in the dark if Chet really wanted to get on a horse. "Let's go up to the barn." Kyle paid off Tubby and pointed up the lane. "Introduce you to the horses."

"Sounds good to me." Chet had a cowboy swagger, his hips rolling as they walked up the dirt yard, their hands brushing. "Lots of things are sounding good to me. I seem to have lost my tolerance for spirits."

"Craig's got a generous pouring hand when a man's been left behind."

"I'll be sure to thank him in the morning." There was

something in the way Chet said it that made Kyle believe him.

"Come on. Let me show you around."

They took a tour of the barn, from one end to the other. Kyle watched the way Chet acted with the horses, the way he knew how to touch them, to talk to them. All in all, he found that he liked the man, which made the whole picture of him with Ricky James even more confusing.

"You know..." Chet was looking at Maze, a nice young chestnut gelding, with an appreciative eye. "I'm feelin' pretty good. If you'd told me last week that Ricky James would leave me stuck a couple hundred miles away from my home without a single word, I wouldn't have believed you. But now I'm just relieved."

"For now, anyway." Kyle leaned on the stall wall next to him, close enough that their arms touched. "You're half drunk and you're in a horse barn. Life don't get much finer than that. See how you feel tomorrow morning, though, when you realize you're still a couple hundred miles from home and he's still gone."

Chet shrugged. "Take tomorrow as tomorrow comes."

Kyle nodded and leaned a little closer. "Seems to me, thinking like that is what got you where you are."

"Partly." Chet nodded and met his gaze. "And part of it was wanting to be something other than what I was. I work with wood all the time. I love wood, I like what I can do with it. I make furniture, and I make art. I carve it, I turn it, I polish it and I feel it. I can tell you what it smells like and what it feels like, and sometimes I can even tell where it was growing before it came to me. But working with wood all day isn't the same as being with something living. It ain't animals or human, and it can get damn lonely."

"I hear what you're saying." There wasn't much else Kyle could say. He lived his life with all kinds of living critters. Some he liked more than others, truth be told, and some he didn't like at all. "Still. Just being around people and horses and dogs doesn't mean you get all your needs met."

Chet's eyes crinkled again. "You got needs, Kyle?"

"Let's just say your needs have had a good run the last few months. Mine, not so much."

"Got laid a lot." Chet nodded firmly. "But I wouldn't say my needs got met. Ricky James, he wasn't exactly a forever kind of guy. I knew that going in, and was glad for it."

Kyle took a step back. "You looking for forever two hours after being left in a bar?"

Chet blinked at him and started to laugh, his head back and his voice filling the barn. It was one of the happier sounds Kyle had heard in at least a month or so. "No, I'm not looking for forever. I'm just talking too much. What I'm looking for is more of the last couple of hours, and maybe some touching added in."

Kyle couldn't even find it in him to be embarrassed. He'd put his foot in it, maybe, and it wasn't exactly polite to back off on a man when he was talking seriously about things, but then... there was beer in them and a few shots, and Chet was reaching out.

Chet had amazing hands, with calluses that hadn't gone away after a few months of not working with wood. His arms were strong enough to turn Kyle right around so he was backed up into a wall. Chet was real close and their hats were in the way, Kyle's brim hitting the wall.

Kyle swallowed hard, suddenly thinking on what Chet had said about holding Ricky James down. "I think that's a fine idea." He looked into Chet's eyes and nodded. "Damn fine." His hat bumped Chet's and then Chet tossed his carelessly onto a nearby bale of hay.

"Do you want something a little nicer than your barn?" Chet leaned in close and pressed hard with the whole length of his body. The stubble on Chet's jaw rasped against his own, and Chet's hands slid down Kyle's arms from his shoulders to his wrists. "Or is here okay?"

"Here is just fine." Kyle was pleased as hell that his voice came out steady. He hadn't been sure it would be, since he could barely remember to breathe. Every bit of blood in his body was pooling in his groin, it felt like, and that didn't leave much for thinking.

"Good, 'cause I'm not sure I'm in a mood to wait." Chet kissed him hard, his hands going tight around Kyle's wrists.

Kyle let Chet be in charge of the kiss; he didn't really have a lot of choice, unless he wanted to actually stop it, which he didn't. He let Chet taste and lick and fuck his mouth, and he might even have let a couple of hungry moans out. And all the while, he was tugging at the hands that were getting tighter and tighter.

He didn't really want to stop and think about why that was making his dick throb.

Their boots were shifting on the dirt and hay, scraping a bit as they started grinding against each other, making rough sounds that mixed in with the heavy breathing and the needy, hungry groans. If the horses cared one way or another, they didn't make a fuss.

With a final yank, Kyle got his hands free. He was so surprised by it, though, that he lost his advantage and was immediately overwhelmed once more. Chet didn't grab at his hands again, but instead went right for his belt buckle.

It took talent to get a big silver belt buckle worked open and a man's jeans unbuttoned and yanked down before a man could come to his senses. Chet was particularly talented.

"Well, hot damn." Kyle's eyeballs almost rolled right back in their sockets when Chet started stroking him. "Gonna embarrass myself."

"Nah." Chet kissed him again and rubbed up on Kyle's hipbone. "Flatter me, maybe. How about we just do this for a few minutes and then I turn you around. Will you let me?"

Kyle groaned and closed his eyes tight, one foot slipping a bit as he started fucking Chet's hand.

"That a yes?" Chet was almost purring in Kyle's ear, his voice full of smooth promises. "I got stuff — learned to carry it with me. I'll take good care of you, Kyle." His hand slipped over and around and stroked and squeezed. Kyle just about went off right then.

"Yeah," Kyle whispered, his balls lifting high, feeling hot. "I'll let you in. Been too long." God, so fucking long. His hole was twitching just thinking about it, and his cock was starting to leak, fast and furious.

"That's the kind of talk that makes me happy." Chet caressed him again, his thumb rubbing over the head of Kyle's cock — and that was it.

"Oh, God." Kyle's head fell back as he came. He let himself make a bit of noise. Why people tried to keep their sounds to themselves, he'd never figure out. Kyle was the expressive type, and as long as his cries didn't spook the horses, that was fine.

When he caught his breath and gathered his senses again, he realized Chet had already moved on a few steps. "Oh, hey. That's real pretty." Kyle reached down and helped Chet smooth a rubber on, taking the time to learn the weight and heft of the man's cock. His balls were shaved bare, soft as anything, and Kyle touched him with something close to wonder.

Chet let him touch, his breath hitching even as he

grinned happily. "You steady on your feet yet?"

"Steady enough. Give me something to hang onto." Oh, Kyle did like the way Chet felt in his hand.

"All right, then." Chet's grin grew dirty and he turned Kyle hard, bending him so he had no choice but to grab the bale of hay and watch his own hat tumble to the ground.

"Oh, God."

"Okay?" Chet leaned over him, shoving Kyle's shirt up and his jeans down, mouthing his spine.

Kyle nodded. "Okay. God, okay." He couldn't really spread his legs for balance and he had all of his weight on his arms and his trembling thighs, but he was totally okay.

Chet backed off for a moment only to come back with wet fingers. "Won't make you hold yourself up long. Promise."

Gasping, Kyle nodded. "Sure. Whatever. Just don't stop. You had lube with you, too?"

"Blister packs were an invention inspired by God and a really thoughtful gay man." Chet's voice was getting as husky as Kyle's, and then the fingers that had been circling pushed in. "How's that?"

Kyle's gasp turned into a groan and he rocked back. "That's fine. Give me more."

Chet laughed. He'd leaned forward once more and the heat of his body, the feel of his cock nudging at Kyle's balls, ramped things up again. "More?" he asked. Kyle felt the stretch as he added another finger.

"Chet, I'm ass up in my barn with a guy I just met. You better fucking believe I want more. I want as much as I can get, as hard as I can get it." It was a long speech, given how he couldn't really breathe at all anymore, but it got him exactly what he wanted.

Fingers stabbed into him, faster and deeper, pushing

the slick in. "That?" Chet demanded, the laughter gone and a hell of a lot more heat added to his voice.

"No. More. Give me your cock." Kyle blushed red saying it, but as his head was down he figured he could pull it off.

Still, he was a bit surprised when it worked.

Chet breached him, the smooth head of his cock feeling completely different from his calloused fingers. Kyle swore and held on tight to the bale. He wanted to shove back and wiggle forward at the same time, his body warring between resisting the invasion and the undeniable need for it.

"Easy," Chet's voice was smooth and soothing, his hands almost gentle as they steadied Kyle's hips. His cock kept sliding in. "God, you weren't kidding about it being a while, huh?"

Kyle took a breath and made himself relax. "Nope."

"Need a minute?"

"Nope." Kyle shook his head, pushed back and squeezed.

"Fuck!" Chet's boots made scuffling sounds as he adjusted his frame, and then he laughed, sounding delighted. "All right, then. Hold on tight, we're going for a ride."

Kyle made an attempt to yell out a "Yeehaw!" but all he could make was more of a whooshing sound as Chet started to fuck him. Over and over Chet plunged into him and pulled him back, dragging Kyle onto the fat cock and stretching him wide.

He had no idea how long it lasted; four minutes, ten, Kyle was mostly concerned with how fast he was getting hard again, and how high his voice was getting when Chet rubbed on his gland.

"There?" Chet at least was getting breathless. "Come on, darlin'. You can do it again." He thrust into Kyle with short, sharp stabs, hitting the spot hard each time.

"Yes!" Kyle couldn't let go of the bale to get to his prick, swinging and bobbing every time Chet plunged into him. He was starting to get tense, starting to feel it in his gut.

"Yes," Chet echoed, and a big hand slipped from Kyle's hip and around to his cock. "That's it. Come on me. Take me with you. Then we'll go back and have a shot and a beer or three."

Kyle started to nod but one of Chet's fingers brushed over the ridge just under the head of his cock and at the same time Chet's prick slammed into Kyle's prostate. "Oh, fuck me, yes!"

Chet growled and shoved in hard, slamming into Kyle's ass until Kyle finally shuddered and started to come, every bit of tension coiled in his belly unfurling and letting go.

He was vaguely aware of the way Chet was holding him and the throbbing in his ass as Chet filled the condom, but mostly Kyle was just glad to be alive, there in his barn, right at that moment.

A shot and a couple of beers sounded fine to him. As long as he could keep Chet over for the night before he headed home, anyway. And who knew? Couple hundred miles wasn't really that far. Maybe it was time to find out about wood and how it was worked.

It wasn't like that could get him in trouble. Trouble had already been through town, and it had left Chet behind. Kyle was okay with that.

The Five O'Clock Bar

Thursday Night Regulars
by Sean Michael

Jason sat all by himself in a booth, nursing his beer, feeling totally abandoned.

Probably because he had been.

Some friends had found out he'd never been to a gay bar before and they'd insisted he had to come see.

So here he was.

It pretty much looked like a normal bar. Except for the fact that there weren't any women in sight.

But there was a bar with a bartender and bottles of booze. There were some pool tables, a bunch of televisions tuned to sports, a tiny dance area, and a bunch of booths. One of which he was sitting in.

Alex and Dave had brought him in, bought him a beer and they'd all sat in the booth for about twenty minutes. Then a pair of hot looking guys wearing leather had come in, Alex had squealed something about "leather daddies," Dave had said "put on your best twink smile" and, with that, they'd abandoned him.

He'd lost track of them about ten minutes ago; they'd either gone into the back or left altogether.

So here he was, trying not to look conspicuous all alone in the large booth, wondering whether or not to stay.

"Pardon me. Do you mind if I share your booth?" Short and lean, graying a little around the edges, the man with the Bud bottle looked utterly out of place. "It's busy tonight."

"No, not at all." Jason waved his hand at the seat across from him. "I didn't start out hogging the whole thing to myself, I swear."

"Thanks, man. I usually sit up at the bar but the bartender says there's two different parties in here, plus the guys watching the playoffs. I should have stayed home." The guy settled, looking a little befuddled. "It's usually quiet in here on Thursday."

It kind of put Jason at ease — not being the only one feeling out of their element. "Is it? This is my first time here."

"You picked a wild one," the man said, smiling over at him before holding out one hand. "I'm Jameson. Jameson Andrews."

"Jason Sealy." He reached out and shook Jameson's hand. "It's nice to meet you."

"Pleased." Jameson sat, fingers wrapped around the beer bottle, peeling at the label.

"So..." God, he was bad at this. Which was probably why he was entirely single. "What do you do?"

At least he hadn't asked what Jameson's sign was.

"I'm a school teacher. Freshman English and the UIL debate team coach. You?"

"Oh, that's cool!" It was. Very. "I'm working at the Book Nook." Managing it, actually, and he was trying to raise funds to buy it. Brenda, the owner, was looking to sell and had promised him six months to come up with the money.

"Yeah? Brenda's a doll. She special orders things for me all the time. What's your favorite genre?" Jameson asked, looking suddenly curious, awake, interested.

"Do I have to pick just one?" Jason felt suddenly like a kindred spirit had appeared in front of him.

"I suppose — this time and this time only — that I can give you two," Jameson teased back, eyes twinkling.

He laughed. "If I can only choose two, it would be historical non-fiction and crime novels."

"I'm a hard-core science fiction fan, myself, although I will admit to a certain fondness for pulp novels."

Nodding, Jason took a sip of his beer. "I like those, too. If it's a book, I want to read it."

"You've got a great job, then. I'm surprised I've never seen you there before. Have you been there long?"

"About four months — I was managing the fiction section at the Borders before that."

He was thinking it was too bad he'd never seen Jameson before.

"Ah. It's not often you hear of someone moving from the big stores to an independent."

"I got lucky. I know Brenda from a book club and so I knew when her manager left her in the lurch, and snatched at the chance to run the place. The big stores have job security but the independents have character, you know?"

It was a topic close to his heart.

Jameson nodded and leaned close and gave him a smile. "I hear you. Job security is cool, but you have to listen to your heart."

"Yeah, exactly!" That smile made his belly flutter some and he returned it. "Can I buy you another beer?" His own was pretty much done and suddenly he knew he didn't want to go home yet.

"I'd like that. Two's my limit, but this is number one,"

Jameson answered, nodding and offering another one of those smiles.

"Cool." He raised his hand and caught the bartender's eye, making the motion for another round.

"So you come here every Thursday night?"

"I do. Every single Thursday for two beers." Jameson chuckled the words out. "Sounds boring, I know."

"Do you meet anyone or anything? Or just come in for the beer?"

"I know the regulars." Jameson nodded toward the bar. "I basically come for the company."

"Yeah? I guess a busy night like tonight kind of puts a crimp in your hanging out, huh?"

"Some. How about you? Are you here with one of the parties?"

"Nah. A couple of guys I know found out I'd never been to a gay bar and thought I should see what they're like." Jason snorted. "Then they found people to go home with."

"Ouch," Jameson said, wincing. "That is not friendly. Do you have a ride home?"

"Nope. But I've got taxi money. My mother didn't raise a fool." He winked, not wanting any pity.

"Shit, we're far enough out that it'd cost you a small fortune. I'll give you a ride, no problem."

"Oh, cool. Thanks, Jameson, that's really nice of you."

This whole gay bar thing was picking up.

Their beers were plonked down and Jason dug out his cash to pay for them. It was the least he could do, if Jameson was going to drive him home.

"Thanks, man. I appreciate it," Jameson said, nodding to him and giving him a warm smile. "So are you from around here or are you a snow bunny that stayed?"

"I was visiting my aunt, actually, and fell in love with

the place."

"Myself, I was born up near the Divide and came to the city for college."

"Oh, it's gorgeous up there, isn't it?" Jason enthused.

Man, Jameson had really nice eyes.

"It is. It's a lot easier to make a living here."

Jason nodded. "I hear that. Still, you've got a nice place to visit for holidays and stuff."

"I do. It's a great place to summer." Jameson drank deep, throat working.

Jason watched, feeling a little warm. Jameson wasn't a hot stud like the guys his friends had left with, but there was something about the man. Jameson was handsome and there was a quiet confidence about him.

"That's one of the perks of teaching, isn't it? Having the summer free."

"It is. I enjoy the time off. I spend my time up in the mountains, believe it or not."

"It sounds idyllic, actually."

Jason half-closed his eyes, imagining being up among all that majesty with no people around, nothing but nature and books.

"It can be. I go really rustic — tents and campfires."

"That sounds like fun. I love roasting weenies over an open flame." Jason put his hand over his mouth. "Oh, man, that sounded dirty."

Jameson's laughter rang out, surprising and full of life.

Jason was rather disappointed they'd both finished their beer; he wanted to keep hanging out with Jameson.

"I don't suppose you'll have another?"

"I can't, but I'd love to go somewhere quieter. Maybe get some coffee?"

"Oh. Okay. That would be great." He beamed at Jameson. He could do that.

"Yeah? Good deal." He got a wink, the toe of the man's shoe against his ankle. "I'm too old for all this noise."

"I might be, too."

He wasn't into all the twink this and leather stud that. But talking to Jameson some more? That, he was into.

"Cool. Come on, we'll go be old somewhere together." Jameson stood, offered him an arm.

"Sounds like a plan." He took Jameson's arm, feeling like king of the world.

And when he passed Alex coming back in, mouth dropping open at the sight of him, well, that put an extra little skip in his step, too.

The coffee was rich and hot. The pastries were flaky and sweet. The company was as adorable as anything.

Jameson was on cloud nine.

"So, tell me — what is the best book you've read this month?" He hadn't met a man that read as much as he himself did.

Jason idly stirred his coffee. "Hmmm... it's a tossup between *The God Delusion*, which made me think a lot, and *Misery*, which I reread every now and then because it always keeps me glued to the pages."

"Man, *Misery* scared me to death. I'm reading *I am Legend*. My honors class is interested."

"Oh, I loved that one. They made a mockery of it with the movie. But then I find that holds true for most books. There's just too much and they don't translate well."

"Yeah, but Will Smith was hot." Jameson winked, grabbed the other half of his turnover.

Jason looked surprised for a second and then laughed. "Yeah, he was at that."

"What? I mean, I know I'm a teacher and need to

keep my academic card, but really, I'm just a big, shallow dork."

"It's a good thing big, shallow dorks are exactly my type then, isn't it?"

"Absolutely." It felt fine, to be flirted with, to be wanted.

Jason's gaze was warm. "So is that what you look for in a movie? Good-looking men?"

"That's a little part of it. I like good dialogue best, though."

"I have to admit, I have a bit of a thing for voices."

"Yeah? Who's your favorite?"

Jameson curled one leg under him, snagged his coffee cup. Shit, this was fun.

"Hmm... it's like books, isn't it? It's hard choosing just one. Lawrence Fishburne is way up there. But so's James Earl Jones and anyone with an accent."

"I like Sean Connery, too. Oh, and that Jude Law guy? Almost too pretty, but the voice?"

Jason nodded eagerly. "Exactly. Liam Neeson, Daniel Craig. Just yummy."

"Tell the truth, you watched *Kingdom of Heaven* with your eyes closed, and drooled."

"Have you been spying on me?" Jason's cheeks were a little flushed and Jameson imagined there had been more than just drooling going on.

"Nope, I just know a kindred spirit when I see him." He winked, chuckling a little.

"We do seem to be well-met, don't we?"

Jason nibbled on his pecan Danish.

"Yeah. I'm glad your friends brought you out." Hell, he was a little glad those friends had dumped Jason.

"Me, too. I'm even gladder they took off, you know? I mean, I don't think you'd have sat with us if we'd been a threesome. So to speak." Jason's flirty, shy smile was as cute as hell.

"Probably not. I'm a one-at-a-time sort of guy."

Jason nodded rather emphatically. "Yeah, me, too. I mean I'd heard of orgies and stuff while I was in college, but I always figured that was more talk than real, you know?" Jason's color got higher and he shook his head. "I'm not sure how we got to orgies."

Jameson's laughter escaped him, loud and from the belly. He couldn't help it; he got tickled.

"You've got a great laugh."

"You think? It bugs some people, I think."

"Really? I like a real laugh, you know? Not one of those little fake-sounding ones."

Jason finished off his Danish and sat back, patting his belly.

"Well, you know, I have to compete with thirty fifteen-year-olds at a time. I have to be heard over them." That was a pretty belly.

"I don't think I could be a teacher. I like books better than kids."

"Oh, I love books, but..." Jameson shrugged. "It's different every day and I like getting to know my kids."

Even the hard ones.

"I think that's great. Teachers mold the future. I know that sounds corny, but it's true." Jason grinned suddenly. "It probably sounds like I'm trying to blow sunshine up your ass, but I mean it."

"You know, that's the weirdest saying, isn't it? I mean, of all the places I've had sunshine, that's not one of them..."

That had Jason giggling, the sound sweet and honest. "I don't think you'd *want* sunshine up there. I mean the burns would be bad. Very bad."

"Exactly. I mean, I fell asleep once up on Cooper Mountain, stark naked. My balls swelled up and blistered.

I thought I was going to die."

Jason's mouth dropped open. "For real?"

"Honest to God. I was a teenager; it was a *mess*. I'd been out drinking with some buddies and things got out of hand." He leaned back, jonesing on the way that Jason listened, on the way those eyes lit up.

"Oh, my God." Looking both horrified and amused, Jason covered his mouth as the amusement won over and laughter spilled out.

Jameson grinned, nodded. "No more tequila for me, man. I'm a walking, talking poster boy against it."

"Everything survived down there, though?"

"Yep. It's all working and functional." He patted his package, cheeks heating.

"That's a good thing." Jason had color back in his cheeks, too. Those pretty eyes met his, though, smiling and happy and, yeah, horny.

"You... Man, this is always the weird part, huh? Trying to see if we want to hook up or take it slow or what."

Jason nodded. "Yeah, but I can tell you that I like you, Jameson. And I think you're pretty hot."

That worked for him. "I have to work in the morning, but I have the weekend off. Would you be interested in having supper tomorrow, maybe? Dessert?" Breakfast?

"That sounds great. It really does." Jason smiled and reached over to squeeze his hand. "Where?"

"I live in Aurora, near the airport." He scribbled down his address on the back of his business card, hand shaking just a little. Man, he'd have to clean. "How do you feel about spaghetti and meatballs?"

"I love spaghetti and meatballs. I'll bring dessert."

Jason took the card, looked at the address and pocketed it.

"Sounds perfect. What time? I get home around 4:30."

"I work until five. I could probably be out there by six. Is that too early?"

"Nope." He should be able to vacuum by then. "It sounds good to me."

It sounded better than good, in fact.

"Cool." Jason bounced a little in his seat. "I can't wait."

"Yeah. You want another cup of coffee?" He could barely wait, either, but there was no reason to cut tonight short already.

"I probably should switch to something without caffeine in it but, yeah, I could sit a little longer."

Jason pulled out his wallet. "My treat this time. It's the least I can do with you driving me around and stuff."

"That works. Thanks." He watched Jason walk away, watched the sway and swing of those lean hips.

Fine.

So fine.

He was going to have something to dream about all night.

Jason was late. Nearly forty-five minutes late. He hoped Jameson didn't think he'd ditched the man.

He'd only been ten minutes late leaving work, but had decided to forgo going home and showering and changing in favor of grabbing a decadent dessert for them at Les Gateaux du Pape and getting to Jameson's on time.

He hadn't counted on the line-up from hell at the bakery. Followed by the most insane traffic he'd ever faced since moving here.

After everything had gone so smoothly the night before it was a little daunting to have everything seem to be against him getting together with Jameson today.

He persevered, though, and finally — at nearly seven o'clock — rang the doorbell at Jameson's little bungalow.

He pushed his hair back off his face and tried to smooth the wrinkles out of his work shirt.

"It's open! Don't let the cats out!"

He pushed the door open slowly, watching for cats and pushing one back with his foot when it made a break for it. He got in and closed the door behind him. "Hello?"

"Hey there! I'm in the kitchen. Come on through." Jameson's house looked... well... a lot like his apartment, really. Books and movies, CDs and electronic equipment stacked on bookshelves everywhere. There was a big cat condo, the wanna-be-escapee cat leaping on top of it, another black face peering out of the bottom.

They made him laugh, in their little home.

He gave them a wave and wandered toward Jameson's voice. "Sorry I'm so late."

"It's okay. I was watching the news. The traffic is deadly. I'm just glad you didn't give up on me." Damn. Damn, a man that didn't suspect the worst immediately? Did they make those anymore?

"Are you kidding? Spaghetti and meatballs with my favorite new guy?" Jason felt his cheeks get a little hot, but he kept going anyway. "I wouldn't miss it for a little traffic."

He held up his box of cake.

"Chocolate mousse cake."

"Oh, you're a keeper." The kitchen was tiny and bright, filled with plants and gadgets and... man, someone liked M&Ms. The tops of the cabinets were stacked with figurines and cookie jars and such.

"You want to put it in the fridge, Jason? There should be room."

"Sure." He opened the fridge, finding it much better

stocked than his own. Which wasn't hard to believe, really.

He found a spot for the cake box, closed the fridge door and wandered the little room, checking out all the M&Ms stuff.

"Can I do anything to help?"

"The sauce is bubbling; the water is heating. You want to make a salad?" Jameson looked good with his little dark hair and goatee, glasses making his eyes look big. Jason decided that he liked the whole relaxed, weekend, faded jeans and T-shirt and bare feet look.

"Sure." He went back to the fridge and pulled out the lettuce, some peppers, and a cucumber. He figured if there was anything that should have been in the salad that he was missing, Jameson could hook him up.

"You got a bowl for me to put this in?"

"I do." Oh. Oh, dude. Look at that ass. Jameson stretched up, grabbed a bowl and Jason's heart almost stopped.

He was still staring when Jameson turned around to give him the bowl.

"You okay?" The front wasn't bad either, but that butt...

Jason blinked and nodded, almost shaking himself like a dog. "Yeah. Yeah, I'm good." He gave Jameson a smile. "I'm really good."

"Yeah? You... Are you opposed to kissing?"

"Oh, no, I'm all for kissing. I think there should be more kissing in the world." Not to mention he'd brushed his teeth at the bathroom at work, just in case there would be some kissing.

"Well, then. I haven't started the noodles yet. There's time." Jameson took the two steps to cross the kitchen floor. "Is here good for you?"

"Yeah, it is." Because if they went somewhere else or

waited, he'd be worrying about it, and this would get it out of the way. Not that it was something onerous he wanted to get over with, but the anticipation was going to kill him if they let it last all night.

He mentally slapped himself and pressed his lips to Jameson's.

Jameson tasted like basil and tomato, garlic and a hint of oregano. Tart and spicy and sweet, all at once.

It was good.

He took a step forward so he could feel the heat from Jameson's body, and their first kiss became their second.

Lean, but not skinny, Jameson felt good against him, felt solid and fine leaning into him. He reached out, hands sliding up the long arms.

Jameson's tongue slipped into his mouth, teasing his lips and making him groan a little bit. He opened up and let Jameson in, his own tongue touching Jameson's to say hi, to invite Jameson farther in.

Jason could get used to this, used to the way Jameson groaned into his mouth, took his lips.

Who knew how long they'd have kept it up if a cat hadn't suddenly started meowing loudly, right at their feet?

Jason broke the kiss, blinking a little, feeling rather stunned. "Is it her feeding time or is she just possessive of you?"

"She likes spaghetti." One thumb drew circles over his jaw. "A lot."

He leaned into the touch, grinning when he realized it was almost making him purr, too. "She can have the spaghetti." He wanted Jameson all for himself.

"Okay, but the dessert is ours."

"Okay." Grinning, holding Jameson's gaze, he leaned in again.

They fit together so well, like they'd been doing this

forever.

It made him smile, which made Jameson's lips tickle his, and so he laughed, arms slowly wrapping around Jameson's waist. They rocked together, hips shifting, sliding together. The man felt good against him, and his cock swelled inside his trousers. He fed a needy little moan into Jameson's mouth.

"I have a big bed. A soft couch."

"Those sound good." Better than spaghetti and meatballs for sure — and he *liked* spaghetti and meatballs.

"Uh-huh. Real good." Jameson turned off the stove and they both started walking, heading for the living room.

He wondered if he should apologize for jumping Jameson's bones as soon as he got in the door, but then Jameson had been the one to suggest the couch or the bed, so instead he slid his arm around Jameson's waist and held on as they walked.

Jameson was an amazing kisser. Jason didn't know if it was because the man was older than the guys he'd dated in the past, or if it was just innate talent. He didn't much care, either. It was all about the kisses themselves and how he could feel them all the way to his toes.

"Damn." Jameson pushed closer, hand on his jaw so they could kiss again.

"I could do this all night." He so could.

"Okay. I bought stuff for pancakes in the morning, if you wanted to stay."

Heat went through him. Jameson was planning on him staying.

"Yeah. I want to. I like pancakes."

"Me, too. Honey or syrup?" Jameson licked his lips.

"Syrup and butter." He chased Jameson's tongue down with his own.

"Man after my own heart..." Jameson groaned, lips catching his tongue, sucking.

Jason jerked, pushing close, his fingers finding Jameson's back and rubbing up and down along it. The kisses threatened to make him crazy, to drive him out of his mind. He hardly even noticed as Jameson sat on the couch, drawing him down, too.

Without even thinking about it, he found himself shifting, rubbing up against Jameson like he was one of the man's cats. From there, it was easy to slip into Jameson's lap, straddle the lean thighs and snuggle in.

The kisses built and built, his slow rocking picking up speed, getting him hot. One of Jameson's big hands was on his hip, moving him, shifting him back and forth, over and over.

For a long time, it wasn't urgent, but then all of a sudden it was and he started tugging Jameson's shirt out of his jeans, wanting skin. Needing it.

Oh, Jameson's belly was pretty — flat and hard, but not ripped. Just his speed. He ran his fingers over it, and then pushed the shirt up along Jameson's ribs. Those long arms went up and the shirt followed, giving him even more skin to touch, to play with.

He swept his hands over the firm pecs, and teased his fingers along Jameson's breastbone. It was the little nipples that kept drawing his attention, though, the little bits of flesh drawing his fingers.

"Pretty," he whispered.

"They're good for more than decoration, huh?" Jameson was panting, staring over at him.

"Uh-huh. Like this, yeah?" He plucked one, teasing and twisting it, watching for Jameson's reaction.

Jason could *see* the blush, the way Jameson jerked. "Uh-huh."

He had a hunch maybe he could get addicted to the

way his touches made Jameson react. He moved to the other nipple, teasing it with his fingertips, watching the little bud go hard.

"Fuck, that's hot." He kept pinching, tugging, loving the way each touch made Jameson cry out.

Leaning in, he took one into his mouth, letting his teeth graze the hard flesh, tongue flicking at it. Jameson tasted good.

Fingers pushed at his jeans, nudging the crotch, rubbing good and hard. It had him moaning and bucking — it felt so good. He closed his lips over Jameson's nipple and sucked, pulling on it with every rub to his crotch. They found a rhythm, touching and kissing and sucking, the heat between them flaring.

He stilled suddenly, gasping as the pleasure built nearly unbearably. "Jeans," he muttered, tugging at his button. He needed to have fewer clothes on. Now.

"Uh-huh." His fly was opened, zipper sliding down.

His cock pushed against his underwear and he moaned, looking up at Jameson, seeing his own pleasure reflected back at him.

Then Jameson's hand pushed into his briefs, wrapped around his cock. Now that was... Oh, hell yes.

He started rocking, his prick sliding through Jameson's hand.

"That's good. You smell amazing." Amazing.

"I do?" He grinned, grabbing hold of Jameson's shoulders and taking a kiss. "Cool."

"You do. Scent is very important. Sexy."

"I want you to think I'm sexy." He wanted Jameson to want him.

He dropped his hands to Jameson's middle, tugging open his top button. Thin and long, that hard cock pushed at the boxers, a spot already forming at the tip. He pushed Jameson's boxers down, fingers sliding over the silky skin.

Oh, he could smell Jameson's need, he *could*.

"More." The lean thighs spread for him.

He rolled his hips, pressing their cocks together, moaning at the heat.

"Better than spaghetti." The words made him chuckle, made him laugh.

"Yeah, much."

He wrapped his hands around Jameson's shoulders and kept moving, his hips rolling and pushing.

One hand wrapped around his cock, gathering both of their pricks together. Jason brought their mouths together, lips pressing to Jameson's as the man's hand slid on their cocks.

He wasn't going to last much longer, not with Jameson's thumb nudging his slit with every upstroke.

His eyes went wide, his prick throbbing and then spraying come up over Jameson's hand.

It didn't take Jameson much longer, stroking his come into that long shaft, before Jameson shot too.

He knew what Jameson meant about the smell now — the scent of their come together filled his nose, made a little shiver go through him as he collapsed against Jamison.

"Mmm. Man. Man, Jason. You are something else."

"Me? I'd say that was you."

Jason grinned, feeling lazy and good all through.

"It can be both of us. We can be something else, together."

"Oh, I like that, Jameson. Almost as much as I like you."

"So long as it's only almost."

He chuckled and snuggled in. "It is. I like you a *lot*."

"Yeah. Yeah, I... I'm lucky that you came in on my have-a-beer day, huh?"

"You and me both." Jason laughed. "I got lucky my

first time in a gay bar. How about that?"

"I'd been showing up for five years. It evens out." His ass was patted, nice and easy. "In the end."

"I'm glad you kept coming back." He wouldn't have. That would have been his one and only time thanks to being abandoned. It was funny how things turned out.

There was a crash from the kitchen and one of the cats went streaking by them.

"Ah. There goes the spaghetti. How do you feel about pizza?"

"Works for me."

This whole date worked for him.

Jameson worked for him.

"Two Bud Lites, Craig, my man." Jameson slid a ten across the bar, nodding to people he knew. Ah, Thursday night. Nice and quiet and normal.

Peaceful.

Wonderful.

"You two want some pretzels?" Craig handed over the longnecks with a smile.

"No, thanks. We're going to get coffee and cake in a bit. Keep the change." He headed over to their table, whistling along with the jukebox.

Jason lounged there, watching him coming, a soft smile on his lover's face.

"Hey, honey. How's the new girl working out at the bookstore? You trust her to close up yet?"

"Why? What have you got planned?" Jason took the beer, lips wrapping around the top of the bottle.

"Chocolate cake and lattes." Look at that mouth...

Jason took a few swallows and then grinned. "I trust her to close up."

One of Jason's feet slid along his calf, the pretty eyes fixed on him.

"Yeah? Cool." They'd moved Jason into his house, letting Jason sell his own place and use the cash to buy the store. So far, things were working well.

Jason's hand reached out, fingers stroking the back of his hand.

"We *could* get the cake to go."

Jameson turned his hand over, twining their fingers together. "We could. We could get ice cream in the drive-through."

"Oh, I like the way you taste when you've had ice-cream." Jason squeezed his fingers.

"Well, then..." They had a plan. Beer. Ice cream. Hot sex.

Jason looked at his beer. "There's no rule that says we have to actually drink these two beers, is there?"

"Nope. I tipped Craig. We have made our appearance."

"Then I think you should take me for ice cream and then take me home." Jason's eyes made him feel like a million bucks.

"I can do that." He tipped his bottle back, drinking deep.

Jason made a little noise and reached out, fingertips so gentle on his neck, on the dark mark on his throat. A mark left by Jason the night before. A soft blush covered Jason's cheeks. "It looks good."

"It does." Jameson was hoping for dozens of them, hundreds over the summer. "Let's go home. You can make more."

"It's a deal."

Jason stood and a big, beautiful stud in leather bumped into him. "Sorry, man, that was my fault. I didn't hurt you, did I?" Man, the guy was scoping Jason out hard.

"No, I'm fine." Jason barely even looked over his shoulder at the guy as he said the words.

"Let's go, J."

"I'm right behind you, honey." He patted Jason's butt, waved on his way out. "Night, all."

The regulars called it back to him, and Jason's arm slipped around his waist as they left.

They headed for the truck, leaning together. He did love Thursdays.

Fighting and Fucking
by Julia Talbot

Good Lord Almighty, if that idiot redneck fuckhead whacked him with his elbow one more time, Sam was gonna rip his head off and shit down his neck.

"You want another shot, honey?" Craig leaned over the bar, his red curls bouncing and glowing in the light. Jesus Christ.

"Yeah. I guess I ought."

Craig leaned back and tucked them curls back off his forehead. He needed a snood. Did the Wal-Mart even carry those?

The little house band had played a set or two and let him sit in for all of it, since Cooter McAllen was down in the jail or down to Shreveport or something. He hadn't played so much in a good long while. Manny didn't pay him or nothing, but he got all the booze he could drink and, shit, a bad night playing music beat a good day roofing.

The bastard beside him bumped Sam again. He growled. "Jesus. Are you blind? I'm right fucking here."

The man turned, slow and deliberate, eyes dark under the brim of a beat-up gimme cap. "Well, if you wasn't so drunk you were weaving on the stool, you wouldn't be hittin' me."

"I ain't drunk; I'm just feeling good." Asshole. "You weren't the size of fucking Godzilla, you wouldn't be bumping me."

The guy was a long, tall drink of water for sure, all legs and shoulders, a trim little brown beard covering his chin. And he had hands the size of Christmas hams. Sam could see that where they were clenched on the bar. "Your momma know you talk to strangers, honey?"

Oh, for fuck's sake. Every over-grown redneck on fucking earth had to notice that he wasn't exactly the Jolly Green Giant. "Oh, sugarbritches, I appreciate your concern. Does your momma know you came down outta the trees?"

"She does. She taught me some manners when I did. Too bad you didn't have the benefit of that education, you little fucker." One big hand swiped up a longneck and the guy took a drink, throat working.

"I ain't that little, Gigantor." Sam slammed his whiskey back, the burn moving all the way down.

Oh, damn. The man stood up. And up, and up. "You're that little."

"Look, just because there's no air up there where you are, asshole..." He was gonna get his ass kicked.

A low rumble sounded. "Look, I was minding my own business, having a beer. I got no real desire to mop the floor with you. Leave it be."

"You kept fucking poking and poking, asshole, and trust me, I'm no big fucker's mop."

A deep breath swelled that barrel chest, and damned if the big guy didn't just shut up and take a swing. Not like a rusty gate, either, but quick as a snake.

Jesus fuck.

Sam ducked, taking it on the ear rather than the nose, which stung like a son of a bitch, but let him sink his fist into Big, Dark, and Bitchy's breadbasket.

The big guy grunted but didn't even move, just plowing right back in to hit him on the back of the neck. Damn, that man had heavy hands.

His right arm went numb — thank God he was left-handed and could get two hard kidney shots in.

"Fuck." It came out low and barely there, but Sam heard the vicious curse anyway, and the fight got dirty all of a sudden.

Somebody had a baseball bat, they had to, because fuck, no man could hit that hard. Sam kept swinging even after his chickens were good and scattered and he'd long lost the ability to focus. Shit, the only way he knew he'd got thrown outside was because it was fucking cold and the gravel smelled like piss instead of beer.

Something heavy and bigger than a breadbox landed next to him, a sharp grunt announcing that the fucking gorilla was on the ground with him. And down for the count.

Okay. Okay, man. Moving.

He was all about the moving.

Except maybe not so much.

"Shit." He could see out of the corner of his eye that wasn't all swolled that his opponent was up on hands and knees, rocking to get momentum to stand. As soon as the big guy was up, he fastened a hand in Sam's shirtfront and hauled him to his feet.

"You okay, man?"

"Uhn." Well, that was supposed to be a yes, but it was close enough. Where the fuck was his truck?

"Shit. Come on." One long arm wrapped around his sore ribs and started steering. "The cops are probably coming."

"Shit." He stumbled along, squinting as the world tilted. "I got a truck."

It was... blue? Green?

"Yeah, because you can see to drive. You look like a hung-over raccoon." They staggered like, well, drunks, weaving through the lot.

"You meet many hung-over raccoons where you're from?"

"Raccoons, low down snakes, and lots of possums..." They leaned against a huge dualie, the big guy fumbling in his pocket. "Where do you live?"

"I got a house over to Fort Collins. A little stucco one." He pointed west, then frowned, turned and pointed a little to the left.

"Jesus. I can't... come on. In." That step was a long fucking way up...

"Goddamn." Sam crawled up, sitting and blinking as he swayed. Wait. Was he supposed to be here?

"Where did you... oh, fuck it." They got moving, the cops coming in the other end of the lot as they motivated out the other. Well, at least they weren't going to get arrested. Sam hoped.

He leaned his forehead against the glass a second; the cold felt good. "Where we going?"

"Home." Well, that was an answer, he guessed. Not exactly helpful, but an answer.

Sam let his eyes close, figuring he'd get his shit together when the truck stopped.

It did, eventually, but, man, it was dark wherever they were. Like middle of bumfuck nowhere dark. Shit.

"You gonna kill me, man? 'Cause if so, I gotta have a smoke first."

"Huh? No. Jesus. Home." The truck door opened, and he heard a hound dog start to bay like it had lost its last friend. Oh, well. That explained it. He was in Hell.

At least he had some smokes. He stumbled down, landing on his knees as he missed the step on the truck altogether. Fuck. Well, okay, he could stay here. He grabbed his smokes from his pocket, squinting as he tried to light one up.

"For Christ's sake." Yanking him up again, the guy took his smokes away, lit two, and gave him one back. "Lula, will you shut up!"

The hound stopped howling and set to whuffling instead.

"Lula?" That was a great fucking name for a dog.

"Lula. She's a coonhound. You okay with dogs?"

The nicotine sharpened his brain just a bit, and his one eye seemed to clear up enough to see that they were at a little hobby-type farm, with a big old house and some fences and shit.

"Yeah. Yeah, I like dogs." He didn't have one right now, not after Wizzer got hit by a truck, but he was fond.

"Oh, good. She'll come barreling, soon as I open the door." Soon as his smoke was skunked that man grabbed him again. Fucking manhandling bastard. They waltzed to the front door like a couple of dancing bears, and in they went, the ecstatic barking of Lula ringing in his ears.

Sam sorta blinked, trying to figure out what the hell was up here. Hadn't he just been drinking? "You got a name?"

"Dermott McEntire." The light went on, spiking right through his eyeballs, making everything blur.

"Dude, that's a mouthful." He found a bit of wall, leaned. "So you a Matt or a Mac?"

"Mac. You? Lula, down." The big dog had pushed right up, paws on Sam's shoulders so she could sniff his face. She gave a little moo sound and dropped to the floor, padding around them and wagging. Cute dog.

"Sam Holly." Shit, that dude wasn't half bad looking, for a giant fucking redneck bastard.

With bruises. And a bloody nose. And a missing gimme cap. The guy had dark brown hair, just a shade darker than his beard. Short, but not buzz cut. Nice wall.

Course, Sam could tell he wouldn't be winning any beauty pageants for a week or two. Maybe three, the way his shoulder felt.

"Come on. You can use the guest bathroom to get cleaned up. Let me just give this old girl a bone..." Mac... it was Mac, not Matt, went and gave the dog a treat, then led him to the bathroom. Surreal.

The water felt damn good. Sam stripped off his shirt, making sure his ink wasn't tore up. Nope, them holly leaves were still there, both sides, but goddamn his shoulder was already turning purple.

Something nosed his ass, and he figured it wasn't the feller, but the dog. Sure enough, there sat the hound, giving him big "feed me" eyes.

"Hey, sweet baby." He sat down on the side of the tub, face leaning against the tile as he gave scritches. "Aren't you just the prettiest thing on four legs?"

Tongue lolling, the sweet girl leaned against his legs, tail thumping on the floor.

"She'll give you new muscles making you pet her, you let her." Mac was watching them from the doorway, shirt off, pair of sweats riding low. "I don't have a guest room. Well, I have two, but I got no furniture in them. You got two choices. The couch, or I got a king-sized bed."

If that was a come on, it was the weirdest one Sam had ever gotten.

Of course, he was really kinda comfortable right here on the edge of the tub, with the pup and the cool tile and shit. "Okay."

The guy rolled his eyes. "Come on, Lula. You need to piss, go ahead and do it before you collapse. I'll be back in a minute."

There went the dog.

He managed to get his business done and get a long drink of water before he realized he probably could see way better if he took his one remaining contact out and put his glasses on.

Oh.

Man.

Way better.

Thank God for hard cases.

"You about done, man?" Yeah, he could see now, and someone had done some damage to that guy's face. He hoped some of it was his.

"Yeah." He was fixin' to just tump over, really, now that the adrenaline was gone and the hurting was coming around the corner.

"Me too." One big hand curled around his waist, pulling him along, the light clicking off as they left. He had a dizzy impression of a little hallway that led to a backroom, and a big old bed, and then he was horizontal and sinking into a down topper.

"Uhn." Oh. Soft. Yeah. That was. Uh-huh.

"Uh-huh. Night."

Okay, so not making a pass. Nope, Mac just rolled over and started snoring, just like that.

Good thing, too, 'cause he was too damn drunk to pretend that he hunted titties and fuck knew he'd kicked enough ass tonight.

Mac woke up with screaming kidneys, a sore mouth, and a terrible ache all over. He felt like someone had taken a baseball bat to him.

Oh, yeah. Someone had.

He rolled toward the bathroom, trying to wallow out of bed. He hit something that felt like a dead body, only warm, and he cracked his eyes open to contemplate someone who emphatically wasn't Lula.

Shit, marthy. That little banty rooster son of a bitch was tore up. Built real pretty underneath the blood and bruises, though.

And that ink was hot. Looked like holly. Wasn't that the guy's name? Something Holly. Mac rolled the other way, grunting when his feet hit the floor. Oh, goddamn, that hurt.

"Shit." Lord, the little fuck was pure redneck.

"You stay. It will take me at least an hour to piss. Then you can go." Creaking, he went to the bathroom, just grumbling and cussing. "Goddamned little motherfucker."

"I ain't that little, fuckhead." No, but the shithead had good ears.

"You're a fucking midget." Goddamn, he was gonna rupture something. His body was telling him something obscene and loud, and by the time he limped back into bedroom, he was good and pissed off.

Man, where had the little fuck gone? He heard Lulu barking in the front yard and the front door swinging shut.

"Well, shit." Mac headed out, looking for the damned fool man. There wasn't nowhere to go.

Lulu bounced over to him, tail wagging like she was the happiest hound on earth. "She needed to do her thing."

Someone was doing his best to smoke around a busted lip.

"Gimme." He grabbed the smoke and took a drag, scratching Lula's ears. "Do you want a hamburger, baby? Huh? Yeah, good girl."

"That ain't your smoke, man." Right, like the little shit was going to take it back.

"Looks like my brand." Mac was pretty sure his pack had been in his jacket, hanging by the door. Or maybe not. Who knew?

"Because only giant-sized crackers buy Camels?"

"Your lungs are too tiny for regulars. Surely you go for ultra-lights." Good to know he could still snark, even with his mouth all crookedy.

"Oh, you son of a bitch." He got a smack, hard enough to sting.

"Fuck. Will you quit that? I got plenty enough bruises without you whaling on me." Lula thought they were playing, and Mac hooted when she romped right against the little guy's crotch.

"Lord, honey. I don't swing that way." The man had good, strong hands. Working man's hands.

"What do you do?" So it was idle conversation. But it stopped him from asking the man which way he did swing.

"Roofing, mostly. Play some banjo on the weekend. You?"

"Finish carpentry. You play, huh? I can pluck a little guitar, but that's it." Those hands would be right pretty on a banjo.

"Yeah. I don't do so good with guitar, but I do okay with the mandolin."

"My daddy could fiddle. He was always disappointed that I didn't have the hands." Mac could make wood sing, though, could make it shine.

"It ain't for everybody. I cain't fiddle worth shit."

"Takes more coordination that I got, I tell you." He

sucked the rest of the smoke down. "It's Saturday. If you ain't got anywhere to be, I'll make us some eggs."

"Okay. You got coffee? I could use a pot or two."

"Yeah. In the freezer. There's a pot on the counter by the fridge." Mac figured he might as well put the little shit to work. "I figure scrambled will be easiest on the mouth."

"Your jaw hurting, honey?" Smart-assed bastard.

"Uh-huh. How's your eye?" Mac'd gotten a few hits of his own in before someone brought out the Louisville.

"Fuck you. It's fine. Lost my fucking contact, though. Asshole."

"You're breaking my heart. I'm pissing broken glass." Funny, though, how they moved easily around each other making breakfast.

"That's the problem with putting yourself in a position to get hammered, man. You end up sore the next day." Man, that coffee smelled good.

"You ought to know." Eggs, toast, strawberry jam. A Snausage for Lula. What else? Mac got the creamer out, figuring he'd need less acid today.

"Shit, I'd've been fine if you'd stayed on one fucking barstool and stopped poking my ass." Mr. Banty Rooster took the cups from him and poured out.

Mac took a deep breath, rolling his eyes to look at the ceiling. "I was not poking you, okay? Just let it go." Jesus.

"Whatever." The coffee at least shut the little fuck up, raw groans sounding as the man swallowed.

Hiding a chuckle in his own cup, Mac sipped carefully, his lip protesting. Damn. That was a bitch.

"I might live. Maybe." One bright blue eye peered out at him from the mass of bruises. "You?"

"Uh-huh. Though my kidneys will probably hate me." Chuckling, Mac poured another cup and headed back to the porch for another smoke.

He'd be damned if the little fuck didn't snatch his cigarette right out of his mouth once he got it lit.

Fuckhead.

He just let it go and lit up another, not ready to fight again. Besides, the sun showed off that man's body real nice. Looked like neither one of them were up for a fight, because Lulu curled up with her head on the little guy's lap, all three of them dozing a little in the sunshine.

That was the way to spend a Saturday, even if he was bruised up like a rotting tomato. It felt good to sit, and he didn't even mind the company, strange as it was.

Mac had to admit, he had a nice view. Sam had a square jaw, a rock-hard belly and a tiny little butt that just begged to be...

Yeah.

Dozing.

Good thing he was hurtin' too bad to spring a boner. That might be embarrassing. Not that hot and tight and tiny was paying him any attention. No, sir.

In fact, the little fuck was sound to sleep, soaking up the rays like it was meant to be.

Lord, lord. Not a care in the world. Too bad Mac had some. He needed to get up and move, get some of the chores done. He'd always wanted a little piece of land, and now he had it, but it sure did make work.

Those bruised eyes opened the second he moved, though, making him take back that whole not-a-care thought. Goddamn.

"You mind hanging until I get a few chores done? Then I'll take you to your truck." Not that he was gonna want to lose the view.

"I'll help. Pay you back for the coffee."

"There's not much, really, just some feeding and cleaning." They could get it done in no time.

"I can handle that. Just point me and shoot me."

"Come on, then." The little barn just had a few stalls, a few feeders, and all they had to do was feed and let the two horses and the donkey out...

For a short little shit, the man could handle a horse, swatting Sorcha on the nose as the old bitch tried to bite.

"You ride?" he asked, needing to fill the silence a little. He was okay with quiet, but it seemed... rude when someone else was about.

"Yup." One of the pitchforks got taken, the little bastard stripping off his shirt to go to work mucking.

With a shrug and a snort, Mac got to work himself, just cleaning out manure and filling water. Okay, so no talking.

"You got any cattle or just horses?"

"I just sold all the cattle." He went through fits and spurts with them. Right now he was too broke for cows.

"They're a lot of work, a lot of trouble." Hay went flying.

"Yeah. I don't mind it, kinda like it, but I just can't afford them..." Mac bit off the rest. This guy didn't need to know about his lack of work.

"No? You said you did carpentry work, man? You ought to do talk to Doug. He's always hunting subcontractors. I'm roofing a whole set of duplexes."

"Doug?" He'd been in a pretty bad slump. Maybe he could just get on for general labor.

"Doug Dillard. Big guy, crookedy nose. If you want, I'll introduce you Monday."

"That'd be right decent of you. Thanks." Hell, if he could get some work that paid weekly he might even make the light bill on time.

"Hell, man, your fist's got my teeth marks on it. We're damn near friends."

A laugh burst out of him. "You know it. Lord almighty." A man had to find his friends in odd places sometimes.

"Yep." He got a wink, or at least he thought he did, it was hard to tell with those eyes so swolled.

They finished up the chores and headed back to the house. Mac started humming, just some old country song he only half remembered. Maybe he could convince Sam to stay for lunch.

When Sam's voice joined his, the harmony close enough to right to shock him, he thought he'd have a damn good shot at it.

Sam groaned, pushed back from the table. They'd slept through lunch, so they reckoned it was time for supper. There was hamburger, rice, soup — enough shit to make a casserole.

It wasn't fancy, but it wasn't bad and it was easy on his sore jaw. "I'll do the dishes." He tossed the paper plates and the aluminum pie plate.

"Thanks." Mac had turned out to be surprisingly good company, relaxed and easy, and not bad to look on, even with the bruises.

"You want to watch the game?" He wasn't in any hurry to get home or back to the bar.

"Sure. Sure, why not?" Mac grinned. "I got ice cream."

"That sounds good." He chuckled, limping on the way to the sofa.

"Lord, we're a pair, huh?" Mac went and got the ice cream, then came on over with two spoons. Those long legs just ate up space, moving Mac across the floor. It was hot.

"Uh-huh." His eyes were focused on the tempting bulge under the denim. He bet that was a nice, long bit of rope.

"Hope you like butter pecan." Settling next to him, Mac scooted close. Close enough to share the dessert.

"I like ice cream, honey. I ain't picky." He took a spoon, moaning as the cold hit his throat.

"Feels good, huh?" They both chowed down, not even turning the game on.

"No shit. My throat feels like I gargled with sandpaper."

"I hear you. And my kidneys." Mac gave him a hard look. "You didn't have to hit me so hard."

"You didn't have to call me short, man. I'm tall enough that my feet touch the ground."

"Your legs go all the way to the floor, huh?" Mac grinned. "Mine go to my neck."

"Naw. There's some nice shit between them legs and your neck." Some real nice shit.

He got a look, kind of sideways and hot as hell. "You could get a closer look."

"You think?" He put his spoon in the carton, shifted a little. "You'll have to take it easy on my poor bones. You tore my ass up last night."

"Yeah. Yeah, I hear that." Still, Mac's hand was sliding on his thigh. "I figure something light. Easy."

"Works for me." He scooted closer. "Something to take the edge off, let us be all melty and shit." Sam could so do melty.

"That's it." One hand strayed right into his lap, pressing against his zipper, just hard enough to make him feel it.

His hand headed for Mac's shirt buttons, giving him a look at that bruised and beaten chest. The guy looked about as horked as he did, but damn, it was still pretty.

Lean muscles. A fine dusting of hair. Ridged belly.

"It's fine. You're fine." He reached out, petting that belly, letting the back of his hand nudge Mac's hard-on.

"Mmm. You got good hands for a midget."

Oh, he was so going to kick Mac's ass. As soon as the man let go of his cock, which Mac was pushing at through his jeans.

"Don't make me beat you again, stud. I'm tired and horny."

"I can go with the horny." Mac leaned right over and kissed him, pressing down against his mouth. A better use for it than sarcasm.

His eyes flew open and he went still for about half a second before he started kissing back, diving right on in and tasting the lingering flavor of ice cream in Mac's mouth. Mac's free hand cupped the back of his head, holding him still. The other one was anything but still, rubbing up against him, hot even through the cloth. Oh, damn. He could handle this. His legs spread, the ache in his cock superseding any bitching from his muscles.

"Mmm. Nice. Wanna see now, huh?" Mac didn't waste any time. The man just started unzipping and pulling and pushing.

His cock jerked, waving like it had a little horndog mind of its own.

"Now, that's pretty." One big hand wrapped around him, Mac feeling him all up and down. A few good strokes had him hard as nails, harder than he thought he could be, as sore as he was.

"Damn, honey, you got fine picker's hands. Fine." He tried to focus his eyes, tried to make his own hands work so he could get Mac's cock.

"Just working man's hands. You've got a pretty prick." Mac was watching, putting his money were his hands were.

"Thanks." His legs drew up a little, right along with his balls. Fuck, yeah.

"No problem." Leaning, Mac worked him harder, faster, squeezing a little.

"I... I can't... Wanna touch you, too. Fuck." He pulled back a little, trying to catch his breath.

"Okay. Yeah." The guy pulled back, long body unfolding so Mac could wiggle out of his clothes.

"Better." He shoved his jeans down, kicked them off. Naked was a much better plan.

"Much. Look at you. Pocket man." It wasn't sarcasm anymore, though. He could tell. It was full on admiration.

He spread a little, hand wrapped around his cock. "Not a bad package."

"Yeah, well. I try." Winking, Mac bent a little, kissing him. Damn. That wasn't bad either. Not at all.

They shifted and scooted until they were touching all over, lips to hips, things just swaying nice and easy.

"Damn. Yeah. More, man. More." Mac was working him, hand moving faster, hips rocking. They were both bruised up as hell, but it didn't matter. Neither one of them was saying ow.

"Yeah." He bit Mac's lip a little, tugging some as his hand slipped down, helping Mac along too.

"Christ." Mac's eyes squeezed shut, and they went to town. Man fucked better than he fought, even, and Mac fought pretty good.

"That's it. Come on, man. Come on and tomorrow? I'll suck you blind." Maybe the day after; right now his fucking jaw was sore.

"Oh, God." Jerking, bucking, Mac came for him, hot and wet and amazing. Just like that. Just because he asked.

He blinked a little, his own need waiting a second,

just so he could watch. For a big son of a bitch, Mac was fucking hot.

Those eyes snapped open again, Mac staring at him. "You, too, man."

"Uh-huh. Was watching." He wiggled a little, got Mac's hand moving again.

"I liked the watching." Chuckling, Mac worked him again, both hands moving on him now, thumbs pressing against his slit.

This sound came up out of him — raw and rough, wicked as all get out. "Again." Come on. One more time.

"Like this?" Mac did it again. Just the same way, making every nerve in his body twang.

"Uhn." That was a yes. For real.

Of course, when Mac did it one more time, everything in him snapped and he shot so hard his teeth rattled.

"Oh, look at you. Damn, honey. Fine." Mac watched him in return, hands moving slow on his skin, rubbing the come in.

"N...not bad for a short guy, huh?"

"Not bad at all." He got him a wink, a kiss. "We could go stretch out in bed."

"We could. I'm a fan, man. Tried and true." Hell, they could go stretch out, then fuck tomorrow, then go have a beer at the club, maybe do a little picking, if Craig was in the mood to let them.

"Sounds good." They eased up off the couch, leaning on each other, natural as you please. This might could work for them.

It really could.

And if it didn't? Shit, they could tie it up a little. Mac was good, fighting or fucking.

The Five O'Clock Bar

No Longer with the Band
by Sean Michael

Jeff Miller had never been so happy to see neon lights in his entire life.

He'd been walking for what had to be hours, his guitar case in one hand and his little duffel containing all his worldly possessions slung over his shoulder.

He'd gotten in an argument with Gil. A big argument about where they should go next and how exactly they were splitting the take. Gil was taking way more than his share — Jeff didn't care one lick if the man was the lead singer, Gil didn't go up there alone every night for damn sure.

But the guys, the fuckers, had all backed Gil, even though it meant Gil continued to get the lion's share while the rest of them split a pittance.

Of course, that pittance would be bigger now that they had one less to share it with, wouldn't it?

The assholes had dumped him out on his butt, van taking off and leaving him in the middle of fucking nowhere. So he'd headed in the opposite direction they'd been going in, heading back for Denver, and hoped like hell there was more along the road than he'd noticed on the drive. It wasn't like he'd been paying that much attention to where they were going, as he'd been busy trying, unsuccessfully, to rip Gil a new one.

Finally, he spotted signs of life. The Five O'Clock Bar.

Jeff dug around in his back pocket and pulled out his wallet. Twenty-six dollars. Well, all right, he had more than enough money for a beer, which would get him off his aching feet and off the road for a while. He could nurse that beer for a long time if he had to.

He ran his hands through his hair and opened the door. Jeff had to blink as he went in, going from the night to the bright welcome of the bar. The noise hit him, too. He'd had nothing but the sound of his own breathing and the very rare car passing by for the last couple hours.

He made his way over to the bar, snagging one of the last stools near the end, and set his belongings down beside him. Oh, fuck, it felt good to get off his feet. Almost good-enough-to-cry good.

"Howdy, stranger. How's it hanging?" A skinny redhead be-bopped up, offering him a beer.

He debated with himself and finally said, "Fine now, thank you," and tipped the bottle at the bartender before taking a nice long drink.

"Good deal. You need anything, let me know."

He pulled the twenty out of his wallet and nodded. "Thanks, man." He couldn't really afford to get shit-faced like he wanted to, but he hadn't eaten since lunch and the beer was likely to give him a decent buzz.

"First one's on the house." He got a wink and a sympathetic nod.

"Oh, you're a prince. Thanks, man." Jeff tilted his bottle toward the bartender in a salute and took a long swallow.

Damn, that hit the spot.

The place was busy enough, guys everywhere — pool table, bar, dance floor.

Wait.

Guys.

On the dance floor.

He started to laugh, the sound building inside him. Of all the gin joints...

"You play that thing?" A lanky blond nodded to him, to the guitar.

He managed to get himself under control. "Yeah. I do. She's my baby."

"Cool. I always wanted to learn, but I don't have the knack."

"You ever tried? It's not rocket science." *Any old fucking idiot can do it*. Gil's words ran through his head. Yeah, he was fucking replaceable.

"Yeah. Shit, I took lessons and everything. I *sucked*."

That had him laughing again. "Jeff," he said, holding out his hand.

"Parker." The man's hand was solid, warm; the shake was strong.

"So you're not a musician, then?"

"Shit, no. I'm an IT tech. Nothing fancy."

"Thank God for that."

Jeff took another drink of his beer, already feeling about a thousand times better than he had ten minutes ago.

Parker laughed, the sound rich and nice. "Man, you hungry? It's two-for-one burger night and I'm starving."

"I could murder a burger, man." It looked like his shitty day was turning the corner.

"Cool. Craig, man. Two burgers, huh? On my tab?"

"And a pair of beers to go with them." He passed his twenty over again before turning back to Parker. "So you're a regular, huh?"

"Yeah. It's a good place. Solid. Safe. Good guys and all." That was a fine little ass Parker had, encased in tight-tight faded jeans. He'd never met a computer geek that looked like him.

"And I take it you're on your own." It seemed obvious, but Jeff'd been in a lot of bars, knew some folks liked to play strange games.

"Huh? Oh, you mean like a steady? I have been in the singles category since November of last year." Parker shrugged.

Their burgers came, making Jeff groan at the smell of them. He was going to embarrass himself speed-eating if he wasn't careful. "That's a great looking burger."

"Eat up. It's good stuff." Ketchup was pushed over with a grin. "You new here?"

"Yeah, my first time." He grabbed the ketchup and added it to his burger, then salted his fries.

Jeff couldn't wait any longer. He grabbed the burger and took a bite, his stomach almost hurting as he chewed a couple times and swallowed.

Parker didn't say much, just ate, foot tapping along to the music, every so often grinning at him.

Jeff made short work of his burger and managed to slow a little with the fries, washing it all down with the rest of his beer.

It was amazing how much better things looked when you had a full meal in you and a bit of a buzz going.

"Thanks, Parker. That hit the spot."

"You're welcome, man. No offense, but you looked a little wild on the edges."

"None taken. It's been a shitty day." It was definitely looking up, though.

"Yeah? You on your own?"

"I am." Jeff nodded. "Kind of got dumped by my band down the road."

"Oh, dude. That sucks rocks. You don't even have a suitcase!"

"Nope. It's pretty much all in the guitar case and backpack."

"Damn. That's tough luck, huh?"

"Yeah. I suppose I should have seen it coming. Gil was always an asshole, but usually the other guys would let us butt heads and otherwise ignore us." Jeff shrugged. He'd find work. He'd do hard labor if he had to until he found another band needing a guitarist.

"Dude. I wish I could tell you I knew about working as a musician, but I don't. Is it hard to find a band?"

"It's finding one that takes paying gigs that's the trick. Something'll come along." It usually did. "I'm guessing IT is a little more stable?"

"Yeah. It's the return for doing code all day. They like to keep you around." Parker grinned and winked.

"I couldn't do that." Go to an office every day? Jeff couldn't think of anything he'd hate more.

"So you live around here, then?"

"I live closer to Denver; I have a little condo. Where's home for you?"

"The last place I stayed at for more than a few nights was in San Francisco. We've been on the road a long time." Jeff laughed a little. "Probably explains why we wound up at each other's throats so much as we did for the last while."

Parker's bright blue eyes went wide. "San Fran, huh? I've always wanted to go there. Always."

"Yeah? It's a great city. Not the cheapest to visit. Or live in, really."

Parker was definitely cute. Jeff itched to grab his ass.

"Denver's not the best, but it's better than California, money-wise," Parker said.

"Anywhere's expensive when you're out of work. I

don't suppose you know of any laborer type jobs going? Hell, I can do sales, even, if I have to."

"I bet we can hook you up with something, man. There's lots of guys here who do construction, landscaping, all that. Hell, Will's got himself a hardware store. Will! Man! You hiring?"

A big bear of a man turned, handlebar moustache fascinating Jeff. "A-yup."

"For real?" This place was like magic.

"Yeah. Money's for shit, but I need someone cutting wood in lumber. You vouch for him, Park?"

Those blue eyes twinkled at him. "I suppose I do."

"When do I start?" Shit, how did he get there? Where was he going to stay? He figured he'd best take the job while the taking was good — he could figure the rest out later.

"Tuesday, huh? Store's closed Sunday and Monday and the little gal that does payroll needs to get you paperwork." One huge ham-sized hand handed him a business card. "Come in around nine."

"Thank you. I appreciate it." Jeff shook that big hand, his own swallowed right up.

Then he shot Parker a happy grin. "That's two I owe you."

"Yeah. Well, there's good karma in helping a man out, although there's a crap side, too."

"My eternal gratitude has a crap side?"

Parker's grin was just wicked. "Uh-huh. I can't come on to you now, because it'd be creepy."

"And I suppose if I came on to you it would seem like I was only doing it out of gratitude?" He sure hoped Parker didn't think so, because that would suck. A lot.

"That would suck, wouldn't it?"

"It would. Would it help if I told you I thought you had a great ass from the moment I first saw it?"

"It would. You should tell me again."

Jeff smiled slowly. "You have a great ass. I noticed it right away."

"Thanks. You've got amazing fucking hands. I approve."

He held them out and looked at them. "Guitar-playing hands."

"Yup. Amazing. What kind of music do you play?"

"Hillbilly rock for the most part. I can pick up pretty much anything, though."

Jeff grinned at the double meaning in that.

"Pretty much. Even... uh... techno?" Oh, man. Parker looked pleased at the pun.

Laughing, Jeff shook his head. "You got me."

"Dude. Want another beer?"

He considered the bills left in his wallet. He was screwed on the food front the next couple days whether he used them or not. "Yeah, I'll get 'em."

"No. I got a tab. You can take me out after a paycheck, yeah?"

Oh, that would work.

He gave Parker a wide grin. "I will do that."

"There you go." Parker waved at the bartender. "Two more, man."

They clinked their bottles together, and Jeff felt himself relax.

"Cheers."

"Yeah. Cheers."

Drinking his beer, he watched the guys moving on the dance floor, fingers tapping out a rhythm on his thigh.

"You dance?" Was that an offer?

"I do. Next best thing to making music is moving to it."

"Yeah? Cool." Parker took a deep drink of his beer.

"Did you want to?" He finished up his beer and left

the empty on the bar.

"Yeah. Yeah, sure."

"My guitar'll be okay here?" He wanted to dance. He really wanted to dance with Parker. He *didn't* want to lose the guitar.

"I bet Craig'd put it behind the bar."

"You think? Cool." He caught the bartender's eye and picked up his case, pointing behind the bar and giving the man his best hopeful look.

Craig nodded, grinned. "Sure, honey."

"Thanks, man."

He put his guitar behind the bar and turned back to Parker. "All right — I'm all yours."

"Do you lead, man? I'm sorta all clumsy." Now he didn't believe that a bit.

"I can start us off."

He fell into position across from Parker, smiling up into the man's pretty eyes. Parker's hand slid over his shoulder, one around his waist. He had both his hands on Parker's waist, feeling the man's hips moving beneath his palms as they circled the dance floor to the ballad crooning out across the bar.

Oh, now. That man could dance, moving easily with the music.

Jeff wound up resting his head on Parker's shoulder. It felt good and he let himself enjoy the heat coming from Parker's body.

"I hope you're not the type to get offended if your dance partner springs a boner."

"I'm more the type to get offended if he doesn't." Jeff grinned, pressing closer.

"Well, then." Oh, someone was hung. Goddamn. He'd have never thought that lanky and lean Parker would feel like *that*.

"You got a license for that thing?" God, that was lame,

but damn, he couldn't just let it go without comment.

"Nope. Never had anyone ask for one."

"Well, it feels very nice." Okay, he was digging himself in deeper and deeper as a nerd.

He opened his mouth and then shut himself up by leaning up and pressing his lips to Parker's.

Parker kissed him right back, hips rubbing that amazing prick against his belly. Oh, man. He wanted a taste of that.

The music changed and he leaned back to look into Parker's face. "There somewhere we can go?" He rubbed himself against Parker, so the man couldn't mistake what he wanted.

"I got my condo. It's about a fifteen minute drive."

"Sounds perfect, as long as we don't have to walk there."

"If God had meant for us to walk that far, he wouldn't have invented trucks."

"Amen." And thank God. Jeff didn't think he could handle much more walking.

He headed for the bar to get his guitar case and his bag, his cock making walking even harder.

"You ought to come back on Mondays, man," the bartender told him. "There's a little group that jams. They're not bad."

The bartender seemed sweet — a little easy-going, but sweet.

"Oh, I just might do that. Thanks, man."

Case in one hand, bag over his shoulder, he turned and found Parker. "I'm good to go."

"Come on, then. I'm around the corner."

He supposed he ought to feel worried, leaving with a guy just like that, but Parker just wasn't scary.

As he started walking, he could hear a horn honking, over and over, his name ringing out. The band.

Turds.

He tossed his stuff in the back of Parker's truck and watched the van slowly come up the road.

"You good, man?" Parker's blue eyes just shone for him.

It had taken them the whole fucking day before they'd gone looking for him. Let them look. He could find another band.

"Yeah, I'm good. Let's go."

"Cool." He got looked at, good and hard. "Let's go dance some more. You can definitely find something better."

"Oh, I'm pretty sure I already have." It had been a long time since anyone had been as nice to him as Parker had in the last hour or so. And it had been even longer since anyone had looked at him like that, like he was the main act and not just a guitarist backing someone else up.

It was about goddamn time, really.

They got into the truck and started moving, heading toward the lights of Denver, the Eagles pouring out of the radio. The man had decent taste in beer *and* music.

Jeff sang along, fingers doing a little air guitar, laughing when Parker caught him at it.

"That is so fucking cool." Parker grinned over, winked.

"I'll have to play for you sometime. But not tonight." He had other plans tonight.

"No. Not tonight. Tonight we've got a completely different game to play."

"We certainly do." He reached over, letting his hand land on Parker's thigh. Fifteen minutes had never seemed so long and, at the same time, the waiting was sweet.

Parker spread a little, hit his blinker and pulled off the highway, heading into a little subdivision full of condos.

Jeff curled his fingers slightly, not enough to touch anything, but giving them both the promise of more.

"I'm just up here on the left."

"Here? On the left?" Jeff slipped his hand up and to the left a little, brushing that huge dick.

"Uh... uh-huh. Fuck." Parker pulled into a driveway, staring over at him. "Right there."

"Here?" he asked again, pressing against Parker's crotch now that they'd stopped moving.

God, the man had a magnificent prick. He couldn't wait to see it in all its glory.

"There. Come inside. I've got a great sofa." Parker arched up a little, pushed into his touch.

"I'm right behind you, man." Well, not right this second. Right this second he was up close and personal, his palm rubbing on denim.

"Mmm. You're gonna make it difficult to walk to the door."

"I should probably stop, then." After all, there was no reason to suck Parker off in his truck when there was a perfectly good condo right in front of them. Still, he kept rubbing.

"Yeah..." Parker's head fell back, throat working.

Jeff undid his belt and shifted closer, mouth finding Parker's Adam's apple and wrapping around it. He sucked gently.

"Oh, man." One hand slid down his back, heading for his ass.

He flicked his tongue across that bit of Parker as the man swallowed. "Fuck. Take me inside, man, before I embarrass us both."

"Hell, yes." Parker unlocked the truck and slid out. "Grab your guitar."

Jeff hopped out the passenger door and grabbed his guitar and bag out of the back before eagerly following

Parker up the lane.

He didn't get a chance to look at the condo. He only got time to drop his stuff and get the door locked before Parker's lean strength was against him.

His back hit the door with a solid thump. It felt good, knowing that Parker was so into him.

He opened his mouth beneath Parker's onslaught, tongue dancing, fighting with Parker's.

That thick, heavy cock rubbed against his belly, making all sorts of promises, making his mouth water.

He slid his hands over Parker's chest, finally finding the man's shirt buttons and popping them open, one after the other.

Soft, curly hair tickled his fingers.

"Damn. Want, huh?"

"Yeah. You got stuff?" He spread Parker's shirt open, tugging the ends out of his jeans.

"Yeah. You know how to use it?" Oh, tease.

He tweaked one of Parker's nipples. "Sure I do. Good hands, remember?"

"Mmm. Damn. I hear you."

He trailed his fingers down over Parker's belly, fingertips pushing into the muscles.

That flat belly went rock-hard, rippling under his touch.

"Oh, God, you are something."

He pushed his fingers lower, fingering the button at the top of Parker's jeans.

"You can have it all." Parker popped the buckle of his belt, the top button of his jeans.

"Yes, please." Jeff licked his lips, fingers itching to grab hold of the prize.

The button fly opened, one pop at a time, that amazing prick parting the denim.

"Oh, look at that." He went down onto his knees,

moaning, rubbing his cheek against the strong heat.

"Oh. Oh, damn. You can look. Touch. Taste. Whatever turns you on."

"You. You turn me on."

He lapped at the broad head, moaning at the scent and the taste. Pure male.

"Oh, man. Sweet mouth." Parker spread his lips, feeding him that fat prick, slow and easy.

Jeff hummed around the thick meat, sliding, running along that thick vein on the underside. Drops fell on his tongue, salty and bitter and male. He began to bob his head, that fat cock spreading his lips wide.

"Oh, damn. Damn, honey. Suck me." Oh, Mister IT was hot, moaning, talking to him. He sucked harder, giving Parker the best damn blow job he knew how. "Yeah. Yeah, just like that. Fucking A."

Jeff hummed, nodding as best he could. Then it was back to sucking and licking and worshipping that amazing prick.

"Soon. Soon, huh?" He could feel it, how Parker was holding back. He wrapped his fingers around the man's hips and tugged, showing he was willing.

"Oh, fuck yeah." There was a bang as Parker's head hit the door, a low cry filling the air as the man shot.

Jeff swallowed Parker down, his throat closing over the head of Parker's prick over and over as he fought to get it all. Jesus, he'd never... The man was so big.

Damn.

When Parker was done coming, he slowly pulled off, licked the man clean. Thick as well as long. So good.

"Fuck, honey. That was fine."

"It was." Jeff reached down and rubbed at his aching prick, groaning.

"You... you want to fuck me, man? I got rubbers."

"Oh, please." Jeff nodded. All that going on up front

and the man was going to let him pitch, too? Life had taken a right turn at good, that was for sure.

"Come on." Parker took his hand, leading him back into a simple little bedroom with a good-sized bed.

"Nice," he murmured, looking at Parker's ass.

"It's okay for now. Bed's comfy." Their clothes started sliding off.

"It's what, or rather who's, on the bed that interests me." He got caught up in watching Parker's clothes come the rest of the way off, though he did manage to get himself more or less naked as well.

"You're fine. I might have to spend the weekend appreciating you."

Parker looked happy, hungry. "I could live with that."

Jeff's prick jerked against his belly, leaving a wet spot, trying for Parker's attention. A bottle of slick stuff was pulled out, handed over, before Parker's fingers wrapped around his cock and started stroking. Groaning, he pushed with his hips, leaning against Parker. "Not too much," he warned. He didn't want to blow the second he pushed into Parker.

The touch eased right away, those fingers gentling. "Better?"

"Yeah. Didn't want it to be over before we began, you know?" His fingers slid along Parker's spine, teasing the top of the man's crack.

"Yeah. Yeah, I want the whole experience."

"Go lie on the bed and I'll open you up."

"Back or hands and knees?"

"You got a preference?" He slid his hand over Parker's sweet ass.

"I don't mind watching." Parker arched up, pushed into his hand.

"Works for me." He liked the idea of seeing the effect

he was having on Parker.

Parker lay on the bed, long legs spread, parted for him, showing everything off. Moaning, he climbed up onto the bed between those legs, fingers trailing on Parker's body. Even only half-hard, Parker's cock was impressive, lying on one long thigh. He stroked it, and Parker's balls, for a moment before he lubed up his fingers and slid them over Parker's tight, little hole.

Oh, damn. Tight. Brutally tight.

"You sure about this?" he asked as he worked a single finger in.

"You know it, honey. I'm real sure."

"You're going to feel so damn good around my dick." He wriggled his finger, and then fucked Parker with it.

"That's a good thing, isn't it?" Parker moved like he danced, riding hard, ass sliding up and down along his finger.

"Oh, yeah. A very good thing."

Jeff worked a second finger in with the first.

"Mmm. Yeah. Yeah, honey. I won't break." He wouldn't think so, not that way the fine man was riding.

"You want more then." He made it three fingers, the tightness and heat a promise.

Parker moaned, one leg drawing up to the skinny chest, hips humping.

Oh, fuck, he needed that.

"Condom?"

"Yes, sir." A whole strip was handed over. Oh, someone was enthusiastic.

Laughing, he tore one off and got it open. He slid the rubber over his cock and then looked up, meeting Parker's eyes with a smile that felt a little wild.

"You're something. Fuck me. I want to feel you."

"You'll feel me." He rubbed the head of his cock against that tight little hole.

"Yeah. Yeah, want to walk bowlegged tomorrow."

Jeff nodded. "You will."

Slowly, but surely, he sank all the way in. Parker braced his heels on the mattress, knees falling open. Jeff panted, meeting Parker's eyes. He knew just when to start moving, the tightness easing up a little.

"Damn. You fill me up."

Parker looked like he was right where he needed to be.

"We fit just right."

He started to move, pushing into Parker with slow movements, trying not to lose it just yet.

"Hell, yes. Just like that, man. Nice and easy."

"You feel so good." Jeff groaned, hips stuttering a little. Taking a deep breath, he held onto Parker's thighs and tried to find his rhythm again.

It was easier than he'd thought, pushing in, rocking in deep and filling Parker up. He moved faster and faster; there was no way he was going to make this last as long as he wanted. He made a grab for Parker's amazing cock, stroking it as he moved. It was filling up nicely, but he didn't need that to know that Parker was with him.

He was still with it enough to experiment, holding harder, looser, moving faster, working to see what Parker liked best. Parker liked a firm touch, that heavy prick filling right up, swelling against his palm. "Like... like your calluses."

Now that was fucking cool. He tightened his hand, moving it slowly to let Parker really feel them.

"Oh. Oh, fuck. Yeah." Parker groaned, hands sliding down his arms.

He closed his eyes, the sight of Parker moving on his cock too much.

"It's going to be soon," Jeff warned.

"Come on, honey. Come on. We got all night for round

two."

"Fuck. Damn." He nodded, his hips snapping hard, and he filled the condom. It was amazing.

Parker's ass rippled around him, pulling the pleasure out of him. He squeezed Parker's cock and bit his lip hard, a moan pulled right out of his mouth.

"You like that." He got another squeeze.

"Yes!" Jeff jerked again, his prick spilling a little more.

"Mmm." Parker kept working and squeezing, massaging his cock.

He shivered, his hand working Parker's cock as ripples of pleasure went through him.

"You're gonna get me up, honey. Damn." That prick was filling, getting harder in his hand.

"Yeah. Give it to me, Parker."

"So fucking hot." Parker moaned, wetting those full lips.

"You are." He leaned in and licked at Parker's lips himself.

Parker caught his tongue, sucking on it, humming softly. Jeff slid his hand up and down that great cock, urging Parker to go for it. All the while, that amazing ass took his cock, riding him, squeezing him. He hadn't even gone soft, so he started thrusting again, nice and slowly.

"Yeah, yeah. Just like that, honey."

It was even better than the first time, his thrusts long — he could feel every inch of Parker's ass as he slid in and out of it. They found themselves a nice rhythm, in and out, Parker watching his every move. He took more kisses, too, their mouths dancing together. They started laughing a little, enjoying it, loving on each other.

He held Parker's gaze, so glad they'd done it like this and not doggie-style. Those eyes were so fucking big, so goddamn blue.

Nothing could last forever, not even this. Eventually his body urged him forward, faster, harder, and he increased his speed.

"F...feel you." Parker was making the bedsprings scream, pushing back up at him.

"Feel this." Jeff pushed harder, banging in hard.

"Yes. Again. Fuck. Again."

He gave it to Parker, letting loose for the second time tonight.

"Damn. Damn, honey... I'm keeping you." Parker's eyes rolled back in his head, long throat working as that amazing prick throbbed, jerking in his hand as Parker shot.

The heat and smell made him moan, and he collapsed on down to give Parker a long, lazy kiss.

Long old arms wrapped around him, fingers sliding down his back. "Spend the night, honey?"

Like he had anywhere to go.

"I'd love to."

He slid out of Parker and dealt with the condom, finding tissues to clean Parker up, too. Then he settled in next to the long, lean body.

Covers landed on him, the moonlight lighting up the room. This wasn't at all how he'd expected to end his evening. Not at all.

He liked this better.

He petted Parker's belly. Much better.

Jeff finished his set and grinned at the regulars giving him a rousing round of applause.

Craig had set him up right; every Tuesday night he played for a couple hours, just him and his guitar. It kept him in form and the guys all seemed to like it. He'd picked up a studio gig or two, and had his ear to the ground for more of that. He was too old to be criss-crossing the country in a van with five other guys, playing at dives for nickels and dimes.

Here, he had a job at the hardware store that paid his bills, and Will was good about giving him a few days off whenever he got a studio gig. And he got to be the star on stage at the Five O'Clock for a few hours every Tuesday. Life was pretty damn good.

His eyes lit on the long, tall drink of water waiting for him at the bar and Jeff grinned. Life was good and then there was Parker, who was great.

"Hey, man."

"Hey, honey. You're sounding like a dream." There was his biggest fan, Parker got off on his music like nothing else.

"It felt good up there tonight." It felt good every night he went up.

Jeff slid his guitar into its case and nodded at Craig, who put a beer down on the bar for him. "Thanks, man."

"Hey. You're making Tuesday a profitable night for me, dude. I'm going to run an ad in the Post for next week."

"Seriously? Cool!" He gave Craig a high five and then turned to Parker, all smiles. "You hear that?"

"I did. Look at you, stud." Parker dragged him in, kissed him hard.

He stepped between those long legs and pressed up against Parker, kissing right back.

"Now, now, boys. Easy with your celebrating." Craig teased and the bar burst into applause.

Jeff reluctantly broke away from Parker's kiss and gave a little wave to the other patrons. Grinning, he took the stool next to Parker and grabbed his beer.

"I was thinking, honey, we ought to go up to Estes Park for the weekend. Wander. If you're not on the clock."

"Oh, that sounds great. I got paid for my last studio gig, so I can even take you out to dinner."

"Mmm. Steaks. I'll buy the beer. We finished that file migration. I'm feeling free as a bird."

"Oh, awesome. Does that mean the grumpies are gone?" He couldn't help teasing, bumping against Parker.

"Fuck, yes. All the overtime is, too, at least until they find us another project."

His hand found Parker's, their fingers twisting together. "That's great. You know, I've said that a lot since that I night I first walked in here."

"Yep. It was a good call, you walking in."

"Fate had a hand in that, I think. Whatever it was, I'll take it. I'll take you."

He gave Parker another kiss. "You want to go home?"

"Let's go, honey." Parker stood, hand around his waist. "See you, man."

He waved at Craig, grabbed his guitar and let Parker take him home.

Right where he belonged.

Crazy
by BA Tortuga

Crazy waved Pistol and Dave off, knowing that, if he let them, they'd stay and fuss and rattle at him and not get on and go. They were heading up to Montana for a week — they had a little cabin and everything.

He was going to spend that week here, looking after things and resting his bones. Frontier Days was a joy, God knew, but nine days straight wore a man's body down.

"Gimme a beer, Craig, and a shot."

One red eyebrow went up. "Another. That's odd for you."

"It's medicinal." Hell, he could sleep in his truck, if he had to. There was a little popup on the back.

"Ah." Craig nodded like he knew something, and passed over the Jack and the Coors.

Damn, that burned going down.

The music was just a shade on the too-loud side, but Crazy tuned it out just like he did at the rodeo, focusing on nothing at all, just staring. Which was why the big hand that landed on his shoulder surprised the pudding out of him. He didn't have it in him for a bar fight tonight, no sir.

"Tim. My God. How are you?"

Not a fight, then. The voice was familiar as hell, and so was that pretty set of green eyes. Buck Williams, as sure as the day was long.

"Well, hell. Howdy there, Buck." Lord have mercy. There was someone he hadn't been expecting. Not even for a minute.

Crazy hadn't seen Buck in what, five years? Not since the man had gone off to working the Texas circuit. He'd been a damned good roper, and everyone knew ropers had to conquer Texas.

"Good to see you, man. I would have known you anywhere. How's it going?"

"Been busy as hell. Still doing my thing. You?" Crazy waved to the open bar stool, fighting the wince when his shoulder protested.

"I'm looking to head back this way." Buck gave him a shrewd look. "Be better if we got a booth."

"I can handle that." Huh. Crazy didn't let himself think too much on it, just got himself to moving.

Buck followed, beer in hand, and settled across from him, grinning a little. "Looks like you're hurtin' some."

"Just the normal shit. Worked Cheyenne — good money, but it's a tough run. When'd you get into town?"

"Last night. Got a hotel room and slept all day." Buck looked good, tanned and lean. Looked tired, too, though.

"Yeah? I drove down this afternoon. You remember Pistol? He's heading on vacation for a week; I said I'd keep an eye on his shit for him."

"Yeah? Well, you always were a good'un." Buck twirled his glass around and around. "I ain't got a right to say it, but I missed you, Crazy."

Crazy chuckled, shook his head a little. Buck had left easy, with a wave and a smile and a fresh-faced kid with a sweet mouth in the truck beside him. Crazy knew what was what. "How's that... Hank? Henry? Howie?"

"Shit. He was gone six weeks in." Grimacing, Buck sucked down his beer. "Lasted about as long as my old gelding."

"Damn." He winced along with Buck, shook his head. "I'm sorry about Tweeter."

He didn't give a flying fuck about Hank-Henry-Howie.

"Thanks." They sat for a minute before Buck gamely tried again. "Want another beer?"

"Yeah. Yeah, I do." One more wouldn't hurt nothing.

"Cool. I'll grab us some." Buck stood up and headed for the bar, still looking fine as frog hair in a pair of Wranglers.

Lord, he'd been stupid for that cowboy, once upon a time. Crying in your beer kind of stupid. Good thing he was over that shit.

Buck looked just as good coming as he did going, not that Crazy was noticing. Not really. He thumped himself a little, reminding himself that Buck'd done left him. That no matter what the man said, he wasn't needed

"Here we go, Tim." Buck gave him a bright smile, handing off a new beer and settling in. "You're looking like a thundercloud."

"Me? Naw, I'm just a little sore and a little tired. Good to see your face, though."

"Yours, too." The silence stretched right out again, the smile on Buck's face fading as they sipped their beer. "I should just let you get back to it, huh?"

"Get back to what? Drinking alone?" The words popped out of his mouth before he could stop them.

"Hell if I know, baby. I don't know what to say to

you." Buck shifted, turning that beer bottle around and around.

"We never were real good at that talking thing." Did he say that out loud? Crazy's cheeks heated, blood rising in his face — and his prick.

"No." Buck's cheeks went red, too, and the man shifted in a whole different way, his Wranglers making an insanely erotic noise on the wooden seat of the booth. "We were always better at something else."

"Yeah." Crazy caught himself with his lips around the mouth of the bottle, damn near sucking it.

Buck stared. "Uh-huh. What?"

"I..." They looked at each other and one of them started cackling, the other one following right on behind, their laughter ringing out.

"Jesus, Tim." Buck sat back, sucking down the rest of that beer. "You've still got it."

"Man's got to have a talent, huh?" Lord have mercy.

"Surely." Stretching a little, Buck glanced at the bar, nodding at Craig. "Want to go get some pancakes or something?"

"You know, I could go for that. You mind driving?" He'd had a couple too many.

"Not a bit. I just started." They headed out together, Buck leading the way to an aging pick-up and opening up for him.

"I was thinking about just sleeping in the trailer, you know. Not risking it."

"Well, we'll figure it out, huh? Coffee might do some good." Buck slid in next to him, and he could feel the man's warmth.

"I ain't drunk, just gone enough that if the state patrol stopped me, I'd be in trouble." Crazy looked around the truck cab, the ropes and CDs and shit. Familiar, comfortable.

146

"Well, there you go." Just for a moment, right after shifting gears, Buck touched his leg, fingers sliding on the denim of his jeans.

Crazy's thigh muscle went hard, just like his cock. "Damn." Oh, Crazy. Hush.

Buck sucked in a deep breath. "I... Yeah. Damn, Tim. You're... well. You get to me."

"Some stuff don't change, I guess, huh?" So long as he kept in mind that this was just fucking, just feeling good. He wasn't sure they could even be friends, not again.

"Yeah. Is that okay? For right now, I mean?" They pulled out on the long stretch of highway, Buck heading for the Waffle House out near Fort Collins.

"Yeah. Yeah, that's cool. Tell me about Texas, man. You like it?"

"It's hot." Buck thought on it a moment. "It's good. I mean, I love it in the spring, when everyone up here is still pissing and moaning about the snow. The flowers bloom and all."

"Yeah. I was in the panhandle for a while. It wasn't bad. I'd melt, though, in the summertime."

"It gets steamy, and let me tell you, cowboy, Christmas makes you wish for indoor arenas." The familiar yellow sign came into sight a few minutes later, promising coffee and waffles.

"I bet. There's some kick-ass ropers that direction, too." Not to mention the bulls. Damn.

"Steers and calves are smaller, too." Buck winked over, finding them a parking place in the nearly empty lot. "Come on, baby. Food."

"Sounds good." The lights were blazing and the smell was unmistakable — years of maple and sausage and eggs on the grill, along with about a zillion pots of black coffee.

They slid into a booth, the little waitress pouncing on

them like they were the best things she'd seen all damn day.

"Coffee, please, ma'am." Smiling easily, Buck charmed that little girl all over, without even trying.

"Two, please." Crazy looked over the menu. He was hungrier than he'd thought he'd be. Hmm. Patty melt or eggs?

"So, how long did you say you were on break for?" Those eyes never left his face, even when the little gal behind the counter wiggled and giggled.

"I'm taking a month. I got to heal up before the race to the Finals, you know?"

"Yeah. I bet you earned it, big time." The coffee was bitter and heavy, but it was just what he needed, and with cream it wasn't so bad.

"It's been a good run this year. Not too many guys getting creamed. Not too many flights."

"Good. You look tired, though." Cocking his head to one side, Buck grinned. "I already say that?"

"Prob'ly. I am. I'm real tired. I reckon this is my last year, full time." Crazy blinked as the words came out of him. It wasn't that he hadn't thought them a lot, he surely had, but he'd never said them.

The expression on Buck's face went grave. "I hear you, baby. We ain't getting any younger, huh?"

"No, sir." He caught himself reaching out and slid his hands under the table instead. "You, too?"

Ropers had lots more years in them.

"Yeah." Flattening his hands on the table, Buck finally let him see what hadn't registered, even with all the bottle twirling and shit. One missing thumb. "I ain't what I used to be."

"Oh, damn." He did reach then, damn the little cook and nosy waitress. "Oh, darlin', no."

He touched the scars, the calluses, fingers looking just

like his eyes. That poor fine hand.

"Oh, I can still work, but competing isn't my strong suit no more, you know?" He got a little grin, Buck's eyes meeting his, a little worried, a lot sad.

"Yeah. Remind me to show you my knee, huh?" Since Buck'd left, he'd had both surged on and one replaced. Still, that wasn't losing a thumb.

He didn't look away; they just stared at each other.

"Okay. You tell me when I can." Buck sounded like he'd swallowed a frog all of a sudden.

"We gotta order waffles first, I think."

"Oh. Well, then." Buck cleared his throat, cheeks hot again. "I'd like the big breakfast thing, honey."

"Cool. Grits or hash browns?"

Before Buck could answer, Crazy reached out with one foot, rubbed up along Buck's leg

"Uh." Poor old Buck's eyes went wide, his mouth dropping open. "Grits?"

"Hash browns for me, a double order, all the way."

This was almost fun.

The waitress finally trotted off to call in the order, and Buck blinked at him. "Tim?"

"Yeah, Buck?

"You, uh. You ain't messing with me, are you? Pity fuck, like?"

Well, now. He wasn't sure whether to get pissed or not. "Fuck off, Buck. I ain't never been that way — I always was straight up with you."

Even when Buck'd gone off with bigger and better and younger.

"I know." Hell, if Buck's ears got any redder, they'd go up in smoke. "I just... well. I'm the one who got stupid, huh?"

"Yeah. Cain't blame you, I guess." Hell, a man started to get old, got wore out, and it felt good to have someone look on you.

"Sure you can." Just like the weather in Colorado, Buck's mood changed, the smile dawning like the damned sun. "I was an idiot."

"Yeah, well, I told you that when you left." Crazy couldn't help but smile back.

Asshole.

"You did. And then some." Their food came and they settled a little, sipping coffee and chewing food as well as the fat.

They got to jabbering and listening to the waitress on the phone, going on and on about jail and fishing and tattoos and halfway houses and how she couldn't decide between her girlfriend or the daddy of her baby.

Lord, lord.

Buck raised one eyebrow at him, all but cackling. "And we thought we had issues."

"No shit. Lord, good thing we ain't complicated and shit, huh?" Just two old rodeo cowboys, that was them.

"That's a nice idea. Just us, huh?" They were down to nothing but sticky syrup and grease drips. Little crumbs of toast.

"Yeah." Crazy looked at the coffee cup, suddenly ready to get the hell out of Dodge. "Where you staying, darlin'?

"Just down the way at the Marriot. You know me and my reward points." Pulling out a twenty, Buck waved at the waitress. "Come on, man. We should go catch up some more."

"I'd like that." Stupid or not, Crazy thought he'd like that a lot.

Buck unlocked the hotel room, calling himself all kinds of a fool. Hell, he'd been pining for Tim, all this time. Took losing his thumb and his career to come crawling back, though. Took knowing he really had nothing else to lose. Which he guessed made some kind of weird sense.

"So. Here it is. Not much." There was one king-sized bed, so if Tim didn't want to do nothin', he'd have to take the little couch.

"It ain't bad at all." Tim sat on the little couch, looking at him, holding that one arm a little careful. "You 'member that nasty old place we got stuck in over in Montana? With the drippy ceiling from the bath up the stairs?

"God, yeah. And the creaky springs that let everyone know what we was doing." He peered at that arm. "You want a hot shower?"

"I ain't got no clean clothes, darlin'. You... you okay with that?" Listen to them, being so careful, so worried.

"Nope. I want to see." Well, there went careful, out the window. Like a dam had broken, he babbled. "Been too long. Want to make sure you're okay. Want to touch you."

Those dark eyes stared him down, looking into him and reading his damn soul. It just went on and on, and then Tim nodded. "I'd like that."

"Oh, good." The relief was kinda crushing. He moved closer, his hand on Tim's shoulder all of a sudden. His good hand. "You're still the same, you know? Still have the prettiest eyes."

Now, look at that blush. "Sweet talker."

"No. I used to pull that shit. These days, I just tell the truth." Sometimes it was just better to lay it on the line.

Tim stood. "Yeah? So, tell me. Did that kid do as good for you as I did?"

"Hell, no. It was the roping that was better there. I told you how long he didn't last." He worked at Tim's collar, then the buttons on that starched shirt.

"Yeah. I just been needing to hear it again." Tim's hands landed on his belly, watching his hands.

"Oh. Well, let me tell you, then. Not a day went by that I didn't think of you. I'm just a stubborn cuss." He pulled that shirt free of Tim's jeans.

"Not too stubborn. You're here." Tim sucked in and his eyes were caught by that six-pack, hard and taut, just like always.

He traced it with his fingers, watching the skin darken. "I am. I can't believe you were just sitting there."

"Sometimes the Lord's good to us." Tim leaned in, lips brushing his jaw.

"Sometimes he is." That was it. That was all the slow and easy he could take. Buck took Tim's mouth, kissing hard, feeling the need rising up.

Oh, hell yes. Tim stepped forward, slamming against him, that belly hot where it was bare. One of Tim's hands wrapped around the back of his neck, dragged him closer.

Crazy. His Crazy, right there against him. Buck closed his eyes and moaned, kissing that man for all he was worth.

Tim's strong, hard body shook a little against him — for *him* — like it was too much to hold in. He could feel Tim's cock, thick and broad, heavy and fat and hard against his thigh.

He reached down to pop the heavy button on Tim's jeans, and damned if he didn't try to use the wrong hand. Cussing, he switched out, finally getting the stiff denim undone.

Tim's cock popped right out, not worried at all about his fucked up hand, his missing thumb, none of it.

Smiling, Buck stroked a little, remembering everything. The weight of Tim's prick, the feel of it. All the same.

Damn, but he had to find out if it tasted the same way, too.

"Damn, no one looks at me like you do. No one." Tim groaned, low and deep, hands opening and closing.

"Never will. I missed you, baby." Dropping to his knees was the easiest thing ever, his cheek rubbing along that hot, silky cock.

"Oh. Oh, sweet fuck. Buck." Tim's hands landed in his hair, petting him. "Please. I want so damn bad."

"I know what you want." Five years might have passed, but Buck knew. He knew how sensitive the spot under the head would be, so he licked right there.

Tim's knees buckled a little, the fingers in his hair clenching. "Darlin'!"

"I got you," Buck murmured, right before taking Tim all the way in, determined to make the man live up to his nickname.

His Tim tasted like fucking heaven, that cock filling his mouth up so pretty. Tim's hips started rocking, just a bit, just a touch. Salty, bitter, all cowboy, and all his. That was Tim. Fuck, it had been so long. His cheeks hollowed, his lips sealing tight as he tried to go all the way down. He could hear all those little swallowed cries falling around him, almost sounding like hurt, the pleasure was so big.

He reached up, pressing two fingers to the spot behind Tim's balls, pushing hard enough to feel.

"Buck!" Tim's hips rolled, bucking once, twice, and then heat flooded his mouth.

Licking and moaning, he swallowed Tim down, his own cock hard as nails. Good. Good enough that he could wait.

"Oh. Oh, fuck. Missed you, missed you so bad, darlin'." Tim's breath was hitching in his throat, voice all husky.

"I missed you, too." Crawling up Crazy's body, Buck

finally got his wobbly legs to hold him so he could kiss that mouth again.

When he did, Tim took his mouth like a marine taking a hill, guns blazing and full force ahead. It was enough to leave him breathless and blinking, his cock drilling a hole against Crazy's leg.

His hips moved, his cock rubbing inside his jeans like to make him insane. "Gonna. Just like this, baby."

"Uh-huh. Just like this." Crazy's callused palm landed on his fly, heel rubbing hard. "I got you, darlin'. I got you.

"Oh, fuck." He humped two, maybe three more times, jonesing on the damned feel of Tim in his arms. Then he came in his jeans like he hadn't since... well, since the first time the cowboy and the crazy clown had made out behind the chutes.

His Tim held on, lips tracing his face, sliding on his jaw, his chin, his cheeks.

"Hey, you." Buck grinned, nuzzling right up on his Crazy. "You willing to give an old fool another chance?"

"I don't see that I have a choice, Mister Buck. You're it for me." One hand cupped the back of his head, fingers rubbing.

"Well, then. How about that shower?" They'd have a lot to talk on, he figured, but if Tim was crazy enough to take him back, he'd settle in and let the man have him.

Never let it be said that he'd make the same mistake twice.

The Five O'Clock was jumping, all of the guys out on the dance floor, two-stepping like mad. Cowboy night, yessir. Crazy and Buck walked in about ten at night, shaking their heads at the crowd.

"You sure you want to do this, baby?" Buck asked, hand in Tim's back pocket. "We could just go home, watch the game."

Tim shook his head, grinning a little. "You think I ain't gonna show off that I got you back? You're the crazy one."

Pistol waved at them from across the way, that wiry hair sticking out all over, the ring where his hat had been pressed down looking silly as hell. "Crazy! Haven't seen you in an age! You coming back on tour with us?"

"Not 'til next year, son. I got me something else to do for a bit."

"Yeah? Hey there, Buck. Long time."

Buck nodded, grinning huge. "Finally came to my senses."

"'Bout time. Buy you a beer?"

"Sure." They settled in, letting Pistol buy the drinks, letting the conversation flow over them and around them. Somehow Tim didn't feel near so old or so tired as the last time they were here, not near so.

Buck was good for him.

Hell, he was good for Buck, and he knew it.

They were getting themselves a place, slow but sure. They'd both had a little put by, and they'd worked a little, and sure enough they had enough to put up a trailer house on a few acres while they built. It was the life Tim had always dreamed of with Buck, even if it had taken him an extra five years to get it.

Hell, he only mentioned the long lost boy toy to Buck once, maybe twice a week. He thought that was real generous of him.

"You settling in again, Buck?" Pistol asked, and Buck chuckled, fingers moving low on Tim's ass, down where the missing thumb wouldn't show a bit.

Not that it ever bothered Tim.

"I am." Buck nodded. "Easy as pie. I got all I need."

Tim kinda beamed, to hear that. He nodded at Pistol, too. "Yessir. We got everything we could want."

He sure hoped it stayed that way.

It would have to. If Buck ever tried to leave him again, he'd shoot the man, pure and simple.

They didn't call him Crazy for nothing.

Hustle
by Chris Owen

Leo stood with his back against the wall and watched the kid playing pool. He'd been watching for about an hour, at first because the leather and denim was pretty and the kid had an ass worth watching, and then because there was something about the way the games played out that made Leo's gut tickle with an uncomfortable memory.

His beer held loosely by his side, Leo had one boot up on the wall behind him, his knee out at enough of an angle that no one stood in front of him to block his view. He'd watched the kid — if early twenties was a kid when he himself wasn't yet thirty — play a series of games, moving between two tables. He was taking anyone who'd have him, which was pretty much everyone. That was likely because he was losing steadily with just enough narrow wins to keep from being laughed out of the Five O'Clock.

Leo drank from his bottle and finished it off. He wanted another one, but if the kid was going to kick into his game and actually make the hustle work, he was going to do it soon. Leo didn't want to miss that; he wanted to be in it.

Leo wanted to save the kid's ass from the shit-kicking he surely deserved, and he wanted to drag that pretty, pretty face out back and go to town on him in many ways that might have been violent but also felt really, really good.

Instead, he pushed off from the wall and went to take a leak, then buy himself another beer. He'd need it, if he was going to watch the carnage around the pool tables. Craig didn't like hustlers much in his bar and at some point a pretty strong deterrent had been laid down; it just didn't happen anymore.

The kid must be from out of town. Maybe Leo would ask. Maybe Leo would get smart and just walk away.

Sure. As if.

A fresh cold one in hand, Leo took himself back to the wall and resumed his position, watching as Dustin LeBray bent way over and took a shot to sink the nine in the side pocket. It was a tricky shot, but he did it, and Leo saw the kid's shoulders relax a bit.

Leo knew what that meant: this wasn't the game where the hustle would kick in. But Leo would lay a bet himself that the kid played better this game than he had all night, losing when it was close. And Leo knew Dustin well enough to know that he'd decline to keep the table; it was about time he headed out to the bar to watch the TV with Craig and a few others before he headed home to his fella, who was getting off work from an evening shift.

So Leo drank from his bottle and kept the fingers of his free hand in his pocket so they wouldn't twitch, and did some math. It wasn't about the game this time, not for him. It wasn't the hustle and it wasn't righteous indignation over Craig's bar playing host to a player in frayed jeans and a worn leather jacket.

It was about the hunger in the kid's eyes. Leo never could resist hunger. The math worked out the way Leo figured it would, and when Dustin inevitably won and shook hands, then declined to keep the table, Leo stepped up.

"I'll take a shot," he said, already picking up a cue.

"Cool. You can break." The balls were already rattling to the end of the table, the kid's quarters feeding the machine.

Leo nodded and waited as the balls were racked up. "My name's Leo." He took another long pull from his bottle and set it aside.

"Zane."

"For real?"

Zane rolled his eyes but didn't look terribly pissed, or even surprised. "My daddy was a fan. Ready to play?"

"Uh-huh." Leo moved around the table, placed the cue ball and lined up his shot. When he looked down the long, straight line of the stick to his fingers, he had to consciously remind himself that he wasn't going to win, he wasn't even going to try to win, and he wasn't going to get lost in the thrill of sinking ball after ball after ball. Hell, he wasn't even sure he could win if he tried his best, anymore. He was just going to manipulate things a little, that was all.

Still. When the balls went skittering and rolling all over the place and three went plop plunk plip, he could feel it in his dick. "Solids," he said, already lining up his next shot.

"Nice break." Zane was watching, leaning on a pulled up bar stool and looking far more casual than Leo knew he had to be. His legs and arms were loose and a smile played around the corners of his mouth.

Leo nodded his thanks and blew his hair out of his eyes. Damn, it was time for a trim. Zane's hair was short, almost military, but not quite. Maybe Leo should try that for a change. Maybe he should just take his shot before he wasted any more time checking out Zane's jeans, or his hair, or his eyes, or his leather jacket. "Where are you from, Zane?" Leo called his shot, took it and missed.

"South." Zane walked around the table to get to the far side and took his shot, neatly sinking a ball in the corner pocket. Leo didn't pay enough attention to see what number. "Actually, just across into Oklahoma."

Leo nodded and wondered when the come-on was going to start, when the hustle would become the point instead of pushing balls around with sticks. Zane had been working it far too long to let it play out much longer. "You're not drinking." It was an observation, not a question.

"Nah, can't play pool for shit if I'm drunk. I'll have a beer later, maybe." Zane took another shot and another ball went softly into a pocket. "Want to make this more fun?"

"I was just wondering when you'd ask." Leo grinned and reached for his wallet. "Twenty?"

"Sounds good to me." Zane nodded, all nice and friendly.

From there, everything went in the expected pattern. Leo won, though he tried not to — Zane's game fell off drastically until it would be embarrassing to play any worse. Leo couldn't be completely obvious about throwing the game, so he had to suck it up and win.

After some back and forth and idle chatter that might or might not have verged on flirting, the bet was upped to fifty on a rematch and Zane's game came back. So did Leo's. It helped that Leo was pretty sure Zane was checking out his ass every time Leo bent over the table to take a shot. Preening always made for better pool shooting, even though Leo tried not to let his ego get in the way.

He won again, unable to resist a rather nice shot that was just too sweet to miss.

The third time the balls were racked, Leo was done with the game and just wanted to take care of the hunger that was glowing in Zane's eyes. He might have played a bit longer — with Zane, and even played a bit more pool — if the heat and want had been more about Leo's ass and less the honest to fuck "I need to eat some food soon or I'll be sick" kind of hunger.

He might not be able to save Zane from whatever had him hustling for money, but he could at least make sure Zane had a hot meal and not humiliate him in the process. Leo knew about that, too, as much as he knew about hustling pool. It was just dumb luck that he didn't do either anymore. Old and knowledgeable at twenty-nine. Who would have thought?

The money on the line wasn't quite a hundred dollars; Leo couldn't afford the full bill, but he'd put up whatever was in his wallet. He didn't miss the way Zane's fingers curled when he saw all those bills coming out, even if they were almost all fives and ones. Leo figured it had been a while since Zane had held that kind of cash.

Leo figured that Zane was going to have to move his ass — Leo didn't have any more money to give, and he wasn't going to let Zane draw this out any longer, either.

Watching Zane shoot pool was a little too much fun, and Leo'd had a few drinks. That sort of thing led to trouble, and he was mostly just trying to be charitable, anyway. Let the kid win the money and then see if they could find a nice motel room to spend part of it on, maybe.

Leo broke hard and started shooting pool like he meant it. He sank four balls off the break and called solids, then gave Zane a tight grin. "Ready to get serious?"

Zane laughed and nodded. "Go, man. Show me your best."

Leo didn't do that — it would defeat the purpose, after all. He showed Zane his B-game instead, with enough push behind it that it looked like anyone else's A-game. Hell, they were drawing a crowd, and a few of the regulars were looking at him with frank surprise.

Leo didn't hustle in his home away from home. Not ever. He didn't even play pool there, usually, just to remove the temptation, so it wasn't a big shock to him that a few of his drinking buddies were looking at him with "what the flying fuck are you doing?" clearly going through their minds.

When Leo finally missed a shot, he only had three balls left on the table and he hoped to hell that Zane's game was as good as he thought it might be. It would really, really suck to have to throw the game and make it look legit after that little display.

Zane gave him a tight grin and chalked his cue. "Nice. You're good."

"I am," Leo conceded with a nod. "I think you are, too, so why don't you show me?"

"Hold tight. You might want to get yourself another beer." Zane's grin grew tighter, a little feral, and Leo tried this best to look unimpressed and mildly annoyed as Zane started sinking balls.

One after another the balls vanished, some shooting hard into the pockets, others dropping softly and oh so slowly, raising the occasional cheer or rueful groan and sigh from the guys watching. Zane took shot after shot, two of them complex enough that Leo had a moment of fright Zane might not make them, but in less than ten minutes Zane was lining up the eight ball.

There wasn't any laughter in Zane's eyes when he looked up to find Leo before he shot, no teasing or flirting.

There was just hunger and pride.

Leo nodded once, just a tiny little nod that was for Zane, and then it was over. He went over to shake Zane's hand, pressing the money from palm to palm. "Good game."

And then the little shit looked him right in the eye and said, "Double or nothing?"

Leo backed Zane into the nearest wall and pressed him there, fully aware that Craig had come to see the tail end of the game and was watching them closely. Leo put his face next to Zane's, close enough to smell his skin and whisper in his ear. "You have my money, Zane. You've got enough for a bed and a meal, and if you plan it right, you can make this hustle get you through to next week. Don't be stupid and don't piss me off. Take the money, get something to eat. Be grateful I'm not kicking your ass for hustling me."

Zane choked out a laugh. "Right. Sure thing. If you don't want the bet, just say so."

"I don't want the bet."

"Aw, and here I thought maybe we were connecting on a spiritual level." Zane shoved him off and stuffed the money in his back pocket. "Thanks for the cash, man. Maybe I'll see you around some time." The contempt was thick in his voice.

Leo sighed. "Yeah." No good deed went unthanked. He moved back and watched Zane stomp his way past Craig in the doorway and on out of the bar. "Can I get a beer, Craig?"

Craig gave him a flat look. "I think someone just walked out with all your money."

Leo grabbed a stool at the bar and put himself on it. "Take my credit card."

A beer appeared in front of him. "I thought you were fucking smarter than that, Leo. Getting hustled? Come on."

Leo gave Craig a half grin and drank from the beer. "Yeah. I'm plenty smart. Thanks for the vote of confidence, though."

"Didn't know you could play pool like that." Craig's flat look had grown a bit speculative.

"Now you do." Leo drank more and watched the TV over the bar, willing to let the conversation end.

"No hustling in my bar."

"Yes, sir."

Craig let him sit and drink, for another three or nine beers, and then cut him off. Leo's head was resting on the bar at that point, so it was probably a smart move.

Then it was suddenly morning, and Leo was home in his bathroom, curled around the flusher with absolutely no memory of how he'd gotten there. All he could remember was a pretty face, a worn leather jacket, and the best ass he'd seen in years.

It took him most of the day to get himself together and back to the Five O'Clock to trade his credit slip for cash. Craig laughed at him, which Leo supposed he deserved, and then he dragged his sorry ass back home again.

It wasn't until the next weekend that his liver forgave him enough to let him darken the door of the bar again, and even then he went right to a corner and stayed there, avoiding the pool tables or even looking around much. He talked to a few souls, had a beer, and set up camp. If anyone wanted to talk to him, they'd find him. He wasn't moving.

He was the Wall of Leo. A rock. An island. A lone wolf.

"Hey." Zane slid into place right beside him, warm and smelling like leather and soap.

He was so screwed.

"Hey," Leo said back. "I'm not playing pool."

"I can see that. You're drinking beer. I was wondering if maybe you wanted to take a walk."

Leo's eyebrows shot up. "To...?"

Zane smirked. "Around the parking lot? Down the road? Hell, even out behind the bar would be good. It's dark out there."

"Why would I do that, now?" Like he didn't know. Like his cock wasn't already heading out there, at least in theory. The rest of him wasn't following, though. Not yet.

Zane leaned in close and spoke soft. "It took me a couple of days to get it. I want to say thank you."

"There, you said it. You're welcome. But if you think whoring yourself out to say thank you is—"

It was a damn good thing he was already against a wall, because the way Zane turned on him would have rattled his teeth. "I ain't a whore." He hissed his words, somehow managing to press tight against Leo despite the fact that they were sitting down.

"Then don't fucking act like one." Leo had to honestly wonder how Zane had lived to be as old as he was. "You wanna fuck, say so. But I don't need your ass or your dick as a thank you. I did good by you — you do good by yourself. You hearing me?"

"Jesus, you're something else." Zane backed off an inch. "Do you seriously expect me to believe you don't want anything in return for letting me win that money from you?"

"For the love of God." Leo rolled his eyes and forced his way to his feet. "Are you always so freaking stubborn and hard-headed? Don't you know truth when it's staring down at you?"

Zane's eyes narrowed and Leo sighed. "I know my truth."

"Then it's time to learn a new one." Leo grabbed

Zane's wrist and dragged him away from the wall, headed out the door. He waved at Craig as they passed the bar, saying, "Be right back."

Craig laughed. Hard.

Outside, Leo kept pulling at Zane until they were around the side and back far enough that even if someone else came out to have some fun, they wouldn't be seen. Probably. "Why are you still here, a week later?"

Zane's eyes glittered. Leo could barely see him, but he could see his eyes shining. "I got a room. I had a hot meal. And then I hired on at the diner to wash dishes. I ain't afraid to work — but I needed food and I needed a bed."

Leo nodded. "Been there. I helped you out, right? I got you money, I tried to do it so you wouldn't even know you'd been played."

Zane's hand landed on Leo's cock, rubbing him through his jeans. "Right. I figured it out, but I see what you did, saving my pride. So what are we doing out here? You're hard for it. For me."

Leo couldn't lie about that, not with the way he was pushing into Zane's hand, rock hard and wanting to rut. "Take some advice. Never blow a stranger as a thank you. It makes you cheap and dirty." He grabbed at Zane's wrist and spun them around, slamming Zane into the side of the bar. "Blow 'em only because you want to."

"You're playing with words. It comes to the same thing."

"Not this time." Leo smashed his mouth against Zane's and took advantage of Zane's surprise to get both their jeans open. When Zane kissed him back, hard and with sharp teeth, Leo wrapped his hand around Zane's cock and started stroking.

Hot and stiff, Zane's prick filled his hand. Leo could feel the coarseness of Zane's pubic hair brushing against his fingers with every draw on his prick, teasing and enticing. When Zane gasped, breaking the violent mockery of a kiss, Leo dropped to his knees in the dirt. "Only because you want to."

"Oh, fuck."

It was flattering, Leo thought as he took Zane into his mouth, that he'd gotten Zane down to two words before even doing anything. He went down on Zane without hesitation, pulling flavor and heat from him, and sucking hard.

When he looked up he could see the light in Zane's eyes again, so he kept looking. Leo sucked and licked and slurped his way over and around Zane's cock, loving the twitches and thrusts and the way Zane was staring, panting a little. Zane's hands were flat on the wall behind him, and his boots were shifting on the hard pack, making scuffling sounds that went right to Leo's balls.

He loved sucking cock in the great outdoors.

When Zane's dick started to leak, Leo reached for his own and started stroking off, his hand flying as little flashes of need shot up and down his spine, making his balls heavy and hot.

"Yeah," Zane whispered. "Suck me. Fuck, yeah. Take it. Come on."

Leo watched Zane's eyes drift closed and pulled at himself faster, rubbing hard at the ridge of his cock. He grunted without meaning to, almost ready to pop, and Zane pushed hard, suddenly fucking his face.

"Shit!" Zane pushed into Leo's face and stayed there for a second, then did it again. "Gonna come."

Leo nodded and swallowed, his balls and dick ready, pressure building.

The nod seemed to do it for Zane and he thrust again, groaning as he came down Leo's throat, the sound of it covering the splash of Leo's juice hitting the ground.

Fire had taken over, lighting Leo up like a torch; he was hot and burning and his body was on overdrive as he swallowed and shot and tried not to fall into his mess.

Zane pulled him to his feet. "That a thank you?" he asked between panted breaths, his face pushed into Leo's neck.

"Nope. That was a welcome to town. Hope you'll stay a while."

Zane laughed softly. "I think I'm going to like it here."

Barney Come Home
by Sean Michael

God fucking damn it, Barn was tired.

Tired and more than a little pissed off. He was angry at a lot of people — and he had plenty to go around. But at the top of his list was whoever had decided that fuel needed to be so fucking expensive. Because of that one thing, he was having to drive extra shifts and shave time off his sleep, and worse, his days off. He hadn't stopped in at home for more than a half day or a night's sleep in what had to be a month of Sundays.

Barn downshifted as he came around the curve, the bright neon of the Five O'Clock right fucking there, calling to him. He had an empty rig and enough money in his pocket to call a three-day truce with the road.

It was just too damn bad that it was only ten p.m. and the man he wanted to spend the night with was working the bar.

He slowed right down anyway and turned into the parking lot. Shit, look at all the cars and trucks. The place had to be jumping already.

He took his truck around back behind the bar, finding

plenty of room at the far, dark end of the lot.

Maybe he should have gone in and showered and taken a nap before going to help Craig close up or something, but he needed to see that fine son of a bitch; he needed a kiss or twenty.

A beer wouldn't go down wrong, either.

Barn locked up and climbed down, heading in.

The lights and the noise hit him hard after the dark, but he knew where the bar was and he made short work of bellying up to it, eyes sliding down to the far end where Craig was working a bottle of Jack, filling a half dozen little shot glasses.

Goddamn, Barn'd missed his ass.

Craig worked the bar, heading his way, filling beers and making margaritas, flirting and joking and laughing.

God, he looked good.

Barney spread his legs on his barstool to accommodate the growing wood in his jeans.

There might have been a bar full of men all around him, but Barn only had eyes for one.

When his favorite redhead looked his way, it was like lightning shooting through him. Craig's smile widened and a frosted mug appeared in the man's hand. "Hey."

Barn smiled, feeling it in his gut. "Hey there."

"You eaten supper?" The beer was handed over, Craig's fingers trailing over his.

Damn.

He turned his hand over, curling their fingers together for a moment.

"No, actually, I haven't."

"There's stew in the slow cooker at the house, or I can get you some pretzels here..."

"If I go back to the house, I'm going to fall asleep, and then I wouldn't get to watch you wiggle that fine moneymaker of yours."

"Have some pretzels and drink your beer." Craig handed over a bowl of salty snacks and went back to work, looking over at him again and again.

By the time Barn was done with his second beer, he was blinking slowly, dozing away where he sat, but not willing to be anywhere else.

"You want to go lay down in the office?" Craig's voice was soft, gentle, and the crush of the bar was gone, all of the sudden. "We just had last call."

God, had he dozed there that long?

"Uh, sure." He gave Craig a lazy grin. "You'll be joining me, right?"

"I'll come wake you up as soon as I'm done. Promise."

"'Kay, babe." He took a lingering, longing look at Craig's lips and hauled himself up off his stool, heading for the little office where Craig did the books and stuff.

The place was neat as a pin, the leather couch waiting for him, pillow on the edge, quilt on the back. Barn sank down, groaning a little as the leather creaked and gave and cradled him like a lover. He barely had the quilt pulled down before his eyes drifted shut and he dozed off again.

He wasn't sure how long it had been before a warm hand was shaking him awake. "Come on, honey. Let's go home."

He wrapped his hand around Craig's arm and tugged him down. "I need my welcome home kiss first."

"Mmm. Welcome home." Craig leaned down, hand landing on his chest as their lips met.

He opened his mouth for Craig, teasing his lover's tongue into his mouth as his hand slid over Craig's, holding it in place.

Oh. Oh, damn, that was what he needed. Craig moaned for him, the weight on that hand getting heavier as Craig leaned, wanting him, wanting more.

"Come on, I won't break." He hadn't felt Craig's weight on him in too fucking long.

"Promise?" Craig laughed into his mouth, settling down on him, cuddling close and making him curse the clothes between them.

"I do, baby. I'll promise you anything you want." His hands slid down, curling around Craig's ass like they belonged there. Which they did.

"Mmm. Tempting." Craig's laugh tasted good — sweet and hot and happy.

Fuck, that happiness was addictive. His Craig loved life.

He squeezed Craig's ass, sliding one leg up over the back of his lover's.

One kiss became another and another, Craig melting down against him.

Tired as Barn was, his prick was still eager and interested, trying to stand at attention in his jeans and get Craig's notice.

"Mmm. We should get you home. Get you in bed..." Craig's leg pushed between his, rubbing. "Let you rest up so you can play with me tomorrow. You are home tomorrow, right?"

"I'm home the next three tomorrows and I'm seriously considering the two after that." If he gave Robertson enough notice, he could probably pull it off.

"Oh, hell yes. I'll call in Ben and Robbie to cover."

Oh. Oh, damn. He'd only had that offer twice in all the time they'd been together, and once had been when his father had had his heart attack.

Someone had missed him.

"Sounds perfect." He brought their mouths together again, sucking on Craig's tongue, his hips pushing restlessly.

They worked it together — simple and strong, just pure need. When Craig's hand pushed in between them, heel rubbing his cock hard through his jeans, he knew he was home.

"Shit, baby. Get me off now and I'll take you to bed and do you right."

"Yeah." Craig slid down to the floor, fingers working his fly open. His cock was battering against the zipper, trying to get out to that pretty mouth, to fill his lover's lips.

A loud noise came out of him as his hands slid into Craig's hair, pulling it from his ponytail. "Please, baby. Fuck."

"Uh-uh. Suck," Craig said, and then that's what Craig was doing, mouth sliding up and down his cock, throat nudging the tip.

"Fuck. Fuck!" Barn couldn't help but repeat the word, the immediate pleasure making his balls ache.

The pressure was fierce and he couldn't stop moving, bucking up into that perfect heat, the tight, wet suction.

"Don't stop, baby." He knew Craig wouldn't, but he still said it, still begged his lover to keep on going, his fingers curling in Craig's long hair and holding on.

Up and down, that mouth gave him everything, Craig starting to moan for him, the vibrations making everything better. He held off as long as he could, enjoying this too damn much to pop too quickly, but finally, he couldn't hold back and long and he grabbed hold of Craig's head, fucking that pretty mouth. Craig opened up to him, letting him all the way in, letting him in deep.

Barn came with a shout, shooting hard down Craig's throat, his hips still jerking when he was done. Craig sucked him dry, mouth hot as hell on his flesh, keeping him hard. He went lax on the couch, feeling boneless and melted. Except for in the middle.

His hands eased up on Craig's head, fingers stroking, petting now as he groaned. "I'd forgotten just how damn good your mouth is, baby."

"Mmm. I hadn't got enough of that." Craig's cheek landed on his thigh, just a little stubbly.

"Don't you worry, baby. I'll make sure you get plenty."

"Come on, There's stew. A bed. A shower. Me."

"Amen."

He let Craig help haul him up, arms going around his lover.

Craig stepped in, gave him a hard hug. "You feel good."

"So do you, man. So do you."

He chuckled and goosed Craig.

Craig jumped and then let him out of the office, heading toward the door. The open door. The busted open door.

"What the fuck?" Craig stepped forward, growling low. He saw the figure move about a second before Craig did, the black shape of the pistol in the man's hands unmistakable.

"Barney, get back!" Craig pushed him back and ran forward, flipping his phone open. "I'm calling 911, you *fucker*!"

"Craig!" Barn swore to God he was gonna kill Craig himself if the man got himself shot.

"Get down!"

He grabbed the first thing that came to hand — a bottle of God only knew what — and advanced. Craig tackled the guy, hands around the man's wrist, dragging it out. Barney was right behind his lover, bringing the bottle down on the thief's head.

The guy went down, dragging Craig down with him. "Fuck. Fuck, Barn."

Barney moved in and sat on the guy's back. "Get the

fucking gun."

"I got it." Craig grabbed his cell phone again. "Are you still there? Then hurry the fuck up. He's unconscious."

"Son of a bitch." Barney's heart was pumping like crazy and he was wide awake now. "Are you hurt?"

"No. No, I'm okay."

The guy moved and Craig kicked the shit out of him, knocking him back out. "Asshole."

"You said it." Barney was growling, staying where he was sitting on the jerk's back.

He could hear the sirens coming from far, far away.

"You're okay?" Craig was panting, he could hear it.

"I imagine I'll live." He reached over and grabbed Craig, tugging his lover in close and devouring Craig's mouth.

They broke apart when the lights flashed in the parking lot. "Okay. Let's get this done."

"You let them in. I'm not moving off him 'til the cops are in here."

He wasn't letting this asshole get another change at hurting Craig.

"Okay. Sit tight." Craig hollered out. "In here, guys. I have his gun. I don't know what you want me to do with it!"

"Put it on the table, sir, and step away."

"You got it." Craig held the pistol out, flat in his hands, obvious, and put it on the table.

"He's the good guy here. This is his bar." Barney watched the cops carefully.

"Yeah. Hey, Craig. Anybody hurt?" A big blond nodded to Craig, smiled.

The other officers came over, helped him up, cuffed the guy that was waking up, nice and slow.

Barney resisted the urge to punch the guy in the face a few times and instead went over to Craig, arm wrapping around his lover's waist.

"What happened, guys?"

Craig looked at Bob, who worked as a bouncer on the weekends. "We were in the office. Walked out and saw the door was popped, and then the guy pulled a gun on us. Barney clocked him with a bottle."

"I wasn't going to let him hurt Craig." Barn was growling, but he couldn't help himself.

"Don't blame you."

The man was awake now, snarling about how he hadn't even gotten to the cash register before he was attacked.

"Get that garbage out of here, would you?"

"Yeah. We need to take a statement, some pictures and all that, yeah?"

Craig nodded. "Sure. We need to see how bad the door's broken, too." Those beautiful eyes met his. "Bet you're sad to be home now, huh?"

"Are you kidding? I'm glad I was here to make sure that asshole didn't hurt my man." He growled a little, tugging Craig in close and nosing along his lover's neck.

Still, he *was* tired and cranky and just wanted all this shit done with so he could take Craig back to the house and they could go to bed.

"Go on home and eat, Barn. Nap. I'll be in as soon as I can."

"I'm not leaving you."

This could have ended so very differently.

"You need your rest."

Craig was starting to vibrate a little.

"And I'll get it. Fuck, we could both use a drink, yeah?" God knew he smelled like booze after breaking that bottle over that asshole's head.

"Oh, God, yes. Get me a Jack and Coke? Please?"

Barn nodded, heading for the bar, glad he still had his boots on as glass crunched under his feet.

He poured himself a shot of Jack and made Craig's drink.

The cops were crawling around the bar and Craig was wielding a screwdriver, working on the door.

Jesus fuck. Welcome home to him.

Then he looked up and caught Craig's eye, his lover giving him a look that just about set his clothes on fire.

Yeah. Welcome home to him.

The sun was high in the sky when Barn finally surfaced from sleep.

Of course, it had been nearly five a.m. before the cops had finished and he and Craig had made it home and gone to bed, so that it was so late in the day was hardly surprising. Barn stretched, groaned, and reached out for Craig. The bed was empty, the sheets cold, and he could smell coffee.

He grumbled and groaned and hauled himself out of bed. Yawning, he headed down the hall toward the kitchen, searching out the coffee and Craig.

Craig was at the kitchen table, leaning over the newspaper, sound asleep, coffee mug right by his nose.

"Oh, for fuck's sake."

Barn shook his head and went over to Craig, bending so he could put one arm around his shoulders. He was pretty sure he could haul Craig up this way.

Craig's eyes popped open, red-rimmed and scared. "Fuck. Oh. Oh, shit, Barn. It's you."

"Hey. Hey, babe." He stroked Craig's back. "It's just me. Come back to bed."

"Yeah. Yeah, okay. Okay, I could do that..." Craig stood up, swaying a little bit. "I couldn't sleep."

"You should have woken me." Barn had a few surefire

ways of making sure Craig slept. He wrapped his arm back around Craig's waist, steadying him as they headed down the hall. "You need your rest. You've been on the road so long."

"Seems to me you need to sleep, too." They climbed back into bed and he pulled Craig close. "You're freaked out about what happened, huh?"

"Nah... I'm good."

Uh-huh. Right. Good.

So good he wasn't sleeping.

Barn slid his hand over Craig's skin. He knew how to make Craig forget everything but him and how good he could make Craig feel.

He rolled over onto Craig, finding that sweet mouth with his own.

His lover opened up, his kiss bitter with coffee and the lingering hint of toothpaste.

He hummed, luxuriating in Craig's mouth, in the sensation of his lover's body beneath his. He'd dreamed of this while he was on the road.

"God, I missed you, Barn. Feels like it's been forever."

"That's because it has been."

He slid his hand along Barney's side, touching, exploring.

"Uh-huh." Craig arched into his touch, the long muscles taut.

"Wanna have your ass, Craig." They really hadn't done that in forever, quick hand and blow-jobs all they'd been able to indulge in for far too long.

"You'll have to get me ready." Craig's green eyes were sharp and needy. "You'll have to touch me."

"Mmmhmmm. Won't that be something."

Barn searched the little drawer by the bed, finding the lube sitting under a paperback.

"A real hardship for you, huh?" Craig rolled closer, licking his ribs.

"Oh, the worst. However will I manage?" He did manage to get the words out before he started laughing, the teasing and the touches tickling him.

His nipple got a playful bite, Craig chuckling. "You're a resourceful guy."

He jerked and rolled onto his back, grabbing Craig up. He pulled Craig up on top of him, fingers smoothing down along the knobbly spine.

"Mmm." He felt Craig's cock throb at the touch.

"*Such* a hardship..." His fingers slid down to tease along Craig's crack, the touches anything but a hardship.

"Mmhmm. A chore." Craig moaned, eyes going heavy-lidded.

"Uh-huh..." He tapped Craig's hole, teasing his lover, teasing himself.

Craig spread, moaning low in his throat.

He touched Craig's hole with each of his fingers before slicking up two. Pressing, he slid one right on in.

So hot. So tight. All his. All his. He moaned, adding a second, watching Craig's face. Those eyes went wide, Craig nodding for him.

"Been too fucking long, babe."

His cock jerked, full and hard, aching.

"Yes. I think I might be a virgin again."

He blinked at that, and then started to laugh, his fingers jerking inside Craig's body.

Craig shivered against him, moaning low.

He let his fingers slide away and rolled them again, putting Craig beneath him. "You can ride me later. This time I want to fuck you through the mattress."

Craig nodded, legs spreading as he grabbed his knees and pulled.

Barney slicked up his cock and lined up with Craig's

hole, rubbing across it.

Craig pushed back, taking him in with a bit of a strangled gasp.

Oh fuck.

Barney closed his eyes and thought of being in the cab of his truck on hour twelve of an eighteen hour day. It was that or pop right away, Craig was so perfectly tight around him. Groaning, he pushed the rest of the way in, sinking down until his hips were pressed up tight against Craig's ass.

"Fuck." Craig grabbed his shoulders, held on. "Oh, fuck yes."

"Gonna be hard and fast, babe. I just gotta have you."

It was all the warning he gave before he started fucking Craig, pounding into his lover.

Craig's legs wrapped around his waist, his lover meeting him over and over, slamming up against him, pushing into him and meeting each thrust.

He dove into it, pushing and thrusting and watching Craig's face as they fucked good and hard.

He'd do this for fucking ever. He would.

"Love you." Craig's words were gasped out, lips open and damp.

"Babe. Yes. Love." Barn was reduced to single syllables, nearly breathless as their skin slapped together.

"Harder. Harder. Fuck. Right there..." Craig's shoulders left the mattress, entire body rippling.

Now that he'd found it, he kept nailing Craig's gland, pounding into the man.

Craig started making the greatest fucking noises, the cries ringing out, filling the air.

"Yeah, babe. More." Barn panted, sweat beading up on his body.

Watching Craig move beneath him, he knew it wasn't

going to take much longer.

He punched into Craig's body again, then felt Craig squeeze him tight. Yeah. Fuck, yeah.

"Do it! Fuck!" he shouted, his hips jerking as he followed Craig right over the edge, coming hard.

Craig whimpered softly, panting heavily, holding onto him as Barn crashed down on his lover.

He managed to find Craig's neck, his mouth opening over the pale skin.

"Mmm. Hey." Craig was almost dozing already.

"Nap, babe."

He shifted a bit so he wasn't crushing his lover, and then settled.

He'd arrange for a couple weeks off when he was awake again — be there for Craig while the man needed him.

He was nearly asleep himself before the thought was even finished.

Barney downed a second bowl of stew, sopping up the leavings with some bread. There was nothing like good, hearty, homemade food after weeks on the road with diner and take-out crap.

Craig was good to him.

He said as much, the words muffled by his last mouthful of bread. "Really good, man."

"Mmhmm." Craig was wandering, humming under his breath, making coffee.

"Oh, hey. I've been making some calls."

He refilled his glass and emptied it just as quickly, the milk nice and cold, the perfect accompaniment to the stew.

"Calls? About what, hon?" Craig poured a cup of

coffee and hopped up on the counter, watching him eat.

"Arranging for a couple weeks off." He gave Craig a grin. "I'm all yours for seventeen straight days."

He'd pulled in every one of his favors, but he'd managed it.

"Seventeen? As in a one and a seven side-by-side?" Craig's eyes were huge.

He nodded, still grinning hugely.

"That's right. A bit more than two weeks. Counting today."

"Oh, man." The hot coffee was carefully sat aside and then Craig gave his spoon a pointed look. As soon as he put it down, he was pounced, Craig rubbing against him, kissing him like there was no tomorrow.

He wrapped his arms around his lover, laughing into Craig's mouth, then giving back as good as he got. Craig was hard, hot against him, each little cry making him want more.

"You gonna ride me right here?" Right here at the kitchen table and then Craig would always think of them together when he was in here.

"Right here. Open your jeans." Demanding, sexy bastard.

Of course Craig didn't have to ask twice. Barn kept one hand on Craig's back, the other pushed between them so he could work his jeans open.

Craig wiggled out of his sweats, sliding his fingers across the top of the almost-new margarine before those same fingers disappeared.

"Oh, fuck."

He got his prick out, shoving aside his jeans as best he could so the teeth of the zipper weren't biting in, and then slid his hands to Craig's ass, spreading the cheeks wide.

He could feel Craig's hand moving, slicking and fucking that tight little ass.

"Babe. Fuck." Just look at the things he missed by not being here.

"Yes. Yes, please. Fuck."

Barn spat into his palm and grabbed his cock, slicking it up a little. "Come on, then."

Craig didn't need to be asked again, his lover straddling him, thighs spread wide.

He guided his cock to Craig's hole, rubbing the head over it before grabbing Craig's waist and encouraging him down.

Craig took him, easy as pie, ass sliding down and welcoming him right in.

"Fuck. Damn. Lover."

He laughed a little breathlessly, meeting Craig's eyes.

"Uh-huh. Love." Those green eyes held his, just sparkling.

He wrapped his hands around Craig's waist, wriggling a little inside his lover before they started to move.

Craig started bouncing on his cock, moving fast and hard.

Shit, Craig was the most enthusiastic, energetic lover. Why did he ever leave at all?

He didn't have to do anything, just held onto Craig's hips, encouraging, bringing Craig down a little harder.

"Good." Craig whimpered, rocked, and pushed down against him.

"Uh....huh." Barn shifted, planting his feet firmly on the ground so he could rock up into Craig now.

"Harder." Craig leaned down, bit his lip hard.

Barn grunted, jerking up at the bite, then gave Craig what his lover wanted, pulling the slim hips down hard as he thrust up.

Craig's ass rippled around him, so tight, squeezing his prick.

"Shit, baby. Gonna make me pop." He wanted to last,

wanted to make Craig lose his mind before he came.

"You won't. Not until you get me off."

"That's right, baby. I swear."

Groaning, he grabbed at Craig's prick, fingers wrapping around the long heat.

He felt that all around his cock, that squeeze, the jerk, the ripple.

He leaned in to grab Craig's lower lip between his teeth, biting and nibbling as his hand worked Craig hard.

Craig moaned, eyes going wide as heat sprayed over his hand.

"Yeah!" Barney shouted, bucking hard as he drove furiously into Craig, letting himself go now that his lover had come.

Craig held on, squeezing him, taking him in and in.

"Craig!" He came hard, the spunk shooting from his balls out through his cock into his lover's body.

"Oh, hell, yeah." Craig kissed him, kept kissing as they floated down.

He held on, arms wrapped around Craig's waist. "Mmm.... seventeen days of this, babe."

"I'm going to be walking bowlegged by the end. I can't wait."

"Yeah, me neither."

He took another kiss, happy, satisfied, and a little smug. And relieved he was going to be here to keep an eye on his lover to make sure no one hurt his Craig.

Halfway through his two weeks at home and Barney was feeling fine.

He'd played some pool, he'd drunk a lot of beer, and he'd made love to Craig until Craig really was walking bowlegged.

He'd also watched that beautiful man hold court behind the bar, serving his patrons, boogying to the music and just... being Craig.

Barn downed the last of his beer and glanced at the clock, grinning when he realized it was almost last call.

The guys that were still hanging on were friends, regulars, playing cards and pool, one couple dancing lazily. It was good.

Home.

He'd made some more calls and found out who was hiring on for local runs. He was ready to give up the long-distance hauls and stay closer, sleep in his own bed with his lover every night.

He hadn't shared the news with Craig. Not yet, but it was there, right under his skin, making him smile.

He nodded to Bob as the big cop started herding the stragglers toward the door.

Craig was starting the cleanup process, his new little bar back working alongside.

It seemed to him that Craig was starting to back off working so many hours, too. It had helped the decision to find something closer to home an easy one.

He nodded to Bob and locked the door behind him, turning to grin over at Craig.

"Hey, you." Craig nodded, zeroing out the register.

"Hey, babe."

He gave the little bar back a nod, but he only had eyes for Craig. "It was a good night."

"It was. They're mostly good, the last few weeks. Come to the office while I count the deposit?" Craig looked over at Nathan. "You holler if you need me, kid."

"Yeah. No sweat."

Barney fell into step with Craig, whistling just under his breath.

"You look happy, hon." Craig counted the cash,

moving quickly.

"I am. I like being here with you."

"It's making my nights go by fast."

"Yeah? Cool. So you wouldn't object to it happening more often?"

"Hmm? Why would I? You're who I want." Craig counted quarters.

"And you're who I want." He moved closer, fingers on Craig's spine. "I'm quitting long-hauling, babe."

"What? Really?" Those big eyes went wide.

Barn nodded. "It was time. I'm getting old." He chuckled. "Truth is, I'm tired of being away from you for days on end, so I found a regular job doing short runs for the Amhurst Dairy."

"Short runs." Coins went skittering across the desk. "As in, you'd be home every night? With me? Together? In bed?"

"Yep." Barn grinned, waiting for it to really sink in.

When it did, he ended up with an armful of happy, cheering bartender, the kiss hot enough to blow his mind. When their lips finally parted he figured his smile was permanent. "I take it you approve."

"Uh-huh. I approve. I more than approve. Damn, hon. I never thought..." Craig was beaming.

"Life's too short to spend most of it wanting to be somewhere you're not, yeah?"

He'd spent too many lonely hours already, and most of them with a man waiting for him at home. Pretty stupid he hadn't done this earlier, really.

"Yeah. Yeah, Barn. I want you here."

"Then here I am. It'll mean fewer luxuries, but you're worth more than the latest electronic gadget, that's for sure."

"We've got what we need." He got another kiss, then another, Craig holding on tight.

"I've got everything I need right here in my arms."

"Then we're gold. Let's close up and go home, Barn. We've got a little celebrating to do."

"Maybe even a lot of celebrating."

He stood and wrapped his arm around Craig's shoulders. Whatever else happened, he was home where he belonged.

Really, it didn't get much better than that.

The Five O'Clock Bar

Contributors' Bios

Sean Michael

Often referred to as "Space Cowboy" and "Gangsta of Love" while still striving for the moniker of "Maurice," Sean Michael spends his days surfing, smutting, organizing his immense gourd collection and fantasizing about one day retiring on a small secluded island peopled entirely by horseshoe crabs. While collecting vast amounts of vintage gay pulp novels and mood rings, Sean whiles away the hours between dropping the f-bomb and perusing the kama sutra by channeling the long lost spirit of John Wayne and singing along with the soundtrack to "Chicago." Check out Sean's webpage at http://www.seanmichaelwrites.com/

Chris Owen

A lover of putting words together since the early days of using crayons, Chris Owen has passed that stage and now uses a computer, which is far less messy. Thankfully, the words go together a little better now as well. The author of several books, Chris Owen writes mainly about gay characters in many different genres ranging from modern day tales to historical romance. How one defines one's family is a common theme in Chris' work, and often the answer is that blood is not as thick as water.

Julia Talbot

Julia Talbot resides in the Texas and has quit her day job. She has a penchant for blank books, gay porn, and big, ugly hats. She can most often be found in coffee shops and restaurants, scribbling in her notebook and entertaining other diners with her mutterings. Julia cut her reading and writing teeth on purple-prosed romance novels, and as a result decided that boys were much more interesting with boys. Intense study of her subject and as much firsthand research as possible figure heavily in her writing adventures. Historical and fantasy settings are Julia's favorites. Her novels include Manners and Means, Jumping Into Things, and Mysterious Ways.

BA Tortuga

BA Tortuga enjoys indulging in the shallow side of life, with hobbies that include collecting margarita recipes, hot tub dips, and ogling hot guys at the beach. A connoisseur of the perverse and esoteric, BA's days are spent among dusty tomes of ancient knowledge, or, conversely, surfing porn sites in the name of research. Mixing the natural born southern propensity for sarcasm and the environmental western straight-shooting sensibility, BA manages to produce mainstream fiction, literary erotica, and fine works of pure, unadulterated smut. Visit BA at www.batortuga.com.

The Five O'Clock Bar

1079947R0

Printed in Great Britain by
Amazon.co.uk, Ltd.,
Marston Gate.